Zalika Benta-Reid is a Toronto-based writer who received an MFA in fiction from Columbia University in 2014 and is an alumnus of the 2017 Banff Writing Studio. *Frying Plantain* is her debut and she is currently working on a young-adult fantasy novel drawing inspiration from Jamaican folklore and Akan spirituality.

'*Frying Plantain* is every bit as delicious as the title suggests' Candice Carty-Williams, author of *Queenie*

'This is the book I've been waiting to read my entire life on the diasporic Caribbean experience. The writing is sharp, intelligent and everything you'd expect from a talented Jamaican writer. I honestly love this book' Symeon Brown

'An incisive and sharp must-read coming-of-age story' *Refinery29*

'Reid-Banks' beautifully written debut follows Kara Davis as she makes her way in Toronto's Little Jamaica' The *i*

'An outstanding debut' *Stylist*

'A show-stopping debut collection, delving into family pressures and control, experiences of identity in immigrant families, and life as a young Black woman in Toronto' *Open Book*

FRYING PLANTAIN

ZALIKA REID-BENTA

dialogue books

DIALOGUE BOOKS

First published in Canada in 2019 by House of Anansi Press Inc.
First published in Great Britain in 2020 by Dialogue Books
This paperback edition published in 2021 by Dialogue Books

10 9 8 7 6 5 4 3 2 1

A CIP catalogue record for this book is available from the British Library.

ISBN 978-0-349-70150-9

Printed and bound in Great Britain by Clays Ltd, Elcograf S.p.A

Papers used by Dialogue Books are from well-managed forests
and other responsible sources.

Dialogue Books
An imprint of
Little, Brown Book Group
Carmelite House
50 Victoria Embankment
London EC4Y 0DZ

An Hachette UK Company
www.hachette.co.uk

www.littlebrown.co.uk

To my mother, Rogene,
without whom none of this would be possible.

CONTENTS

PIG HEAD

ON MY FIRST VISIT TO JAMAICA I SAW A PIG'S severed head. My grandmother's sister Auntie had asked me to grab two bottles of Ting from the icebox and when I walked into the kitchen and pulled up the icebox lid there it was, its blood splattered and frozen thick on the bottles beneath it, its brown tongue lolling out from between its clenched teeth, the tip making a small dip in the ice water.

My cousins were in the next room, so I clamped my palm over my mouth to keep from screaming. They were all my age or younger, and during the five days I'd already been in Hanover they'd all spoken easily about the chickens they strangled for soup and they'd idly thrown stones at alligators for sport, side-eyeing me when I was too afraid to join in. I wanted to avoid a repeat of those looks, so I bit down on my finger to push the scream back down my throat.

Only two days before I'd squealed when Rodney, who was ten like me, had wrung a chicken's neck without warning; the jerk of his hands and the quick snap of the bone had made me fall back against the coops behind me. He turned to me after I'd silenced myself and his mouth and nose were twisted up as if he was deciding whether he was irritated with me or contemptuous or just amused.

"Ah wah?" he asked. "Yuh nuh cook soup in Canada?"

"Sure we do," I said, my voice a mumble. "The chicken is just dead first."

He didn't respond, and he didn't say anything about it in front of our other cousins; but soon after, they all treated me with a new-found delicacy. When the girls played Dandy Shandy with their friends they stopped asking me to be in the middle, and when all of them climbed trees to pluck ripe mangoes they no longer hung, loose-limbed, from the branches and tried to convince me to clamber up and join them. For the first three days of my visit, they'd at least tease me, broad smiles stretching their cheeks, and yell down, "This tree frighten yuh like how duppy frighten yuh?" Then they'd let leaves fall from their hands onto my hair and laugh when I tried to pick them out of my plaits. I'd fuss and grumble, piqued at the taunting but grateful for the inclusion, for being thought tough enough to handle the same mockery they inflicted on each other. But after the chicken, they didn't goad me anymore and they only approached me for games like tag, for games they thought Canadian girls could stomach.

"What's taking you so long?" My mother came up behind me and instead of waiting for me to answer, leaned forward and peered into the icebox, swallowing hard as she did. "Great," she whispered. "Are you going to be traumatized by this?"

I didn't quite know what she meant — but I felt like the right answer was no, so I shook my head. My mother was like my cousins. I hadn't seen her butcher any animals, but back home she stepped on spiders without flinching and she cussed out men who tried to reach for her in the street, and I couldn't bear her scoffing at me for screaming at a pig's head.

"Eloise!" Nana called. My grandmother came into the kitchen from the backyard and stood next to us, her hands on her hips. The deep arch in her back made her breasts and belly protrude, and the way she stood with her legs apart reminded me of a pigeon.

"I hear Auntie call out she want a drink from the fridge. That there is the freezer, yuh nuh want that.

Yuh know wah Bredda put in there? Kara canna see that, she nuh raise up for it."

"I closed the lid," said my mother. "Anyway, it was a pig's head. It's not like she saw the pig get slaughtered. She's fine."

"Kara's a soft one. She canna handle these things."

I felt my mother take a deep breath in, and I suddenly became aware of all the exposed knives in the kitchen and wondered if there was any way I could hide them without being noticed. We were only here for ten days and my mother and Nana had already gotten into two fights—one in the airport on the day we landed, the other, two nights after—and Auntie had threatened to set the dogs on them if they didn't calm down.

"Mi thought Canada was supposed fi be a civilized place, how yuh two fight like the dogs them? Cha."

I wondered if all daughters fought with their mothers this way when they grew up, and I started to tear up just thinking about it. Nana looked at me.

"See? She ah cry about the head."

"It's not about the head," said my mother. "She just cries over anything."

"Like I say. She a soft chile."

. . .

THE PIG'S HEAD haunted me for the rest of the trip. When we did things the tourists did, like try to climb up the Dunn's River Falls, I'd imagine the head waiting for me at the top of the rocks, the blue-white water pouring out of its snout and ears; and at Auntie's house, I was haunted by its disappearance and legacy. Nana kept me away from the kitchen and either icebox. Her normally pinched-up face was smooth with concern, which irritated me more than it comforted me.

But back home in Toronto, I told everyone about the head. At school during recess, I gathered all of my classmates around in the playground and watched as their pink faces flushed red with vicarious thrill.

"And you killed the pig?" They gasped. "You weren't scared?"

"You weren't grossed out?"

"Nope," I said without hesitation. "It was cool."

"Was there lots of blood?"

"Tons!" I giggled and leaned in so everyone around me could make the circle tighter. "I was the one who stuck it in the throat and the blood just came gushing out."

"Eew!" they sang out, covering their faces, cowering from the image of spurting blood, dark and thick, and a slashed throat. They spread their hands out so they could see me through the spaces between their fingers.

"Did any of the blood get on you?"

"Yeah. That part was pretty bad." The words came naturally, and with every sentence I could see the images of my story unfold before me like they were pieces of a memory I'd forgotten. I told many stories at school. Stories that made me the subject of interest; stories that took on lives of their own and allowed me to build different identities, personalities; stories that brought me audiences.

The only person who wasn't all that excited about the pig's head was Anna Mae, a girl one grade above us who always had her blonde hair twisted into French braids. She'd just moved to the city from a farm in Kapuskasing—somewhere in Northern Ontario—and she'd already told us about the blind or sickly kittens they would drown in the river there. For the first couple of months she was known as the girl who killed cats, and whenever she showed up at a birthday party (the birthday boy or girl having been guilted into inviting her by his or her parents), if there was a cat in the house, all of the kids would take turns holding it tightly to their chests or someone would lock it away in the basement for safety, always keeping an eye on Anna Mae and what she doing, where she was going.

But away from school, in the neighbourhood where we lived, the kids were as skeptical of my story as Anna

Mae was unenthused, staring blankly at me as she had. Most of my neighbourhood friends had either just moved here from the Islands or had visited them so often it was like they lived both here and there. And so none of them found anything intriguing about my story—not even the kids who came from the Island cities and not the farms. I wasn't foolish enough to tell them I'd stuck the pig, though—I knew if I pushed it too far, they'd find me out, and their trust would be much harder to win back than that of the white kids at school.

"So what *did* you do, then?"

We were at Jordan's apartment, in her bedroom, sucking on jumbo-sized freezies and deciding which CD to play in the Sony stereo: *Rule 3:36* or *The Marshall Mathers LP*. I was on the bed and lying on my back, my head dangling off the foot of the mattress, almost touching the floor, my eyes on the pink paint-chipped walls and the Destiny's Child and Aaliyah posters.

"I watched," I said.

Rochelle, who was sitting at the study desk in the corner of the room, logged in to a chat room, turned away from the computer, and looked at me. "Did you close your eyes?"

"No. I saw the whole thing."

"And you weren't scared?" said Jordan, inching closer to where I was lying down.

"Nope."

"Yeah, right."

"It's true! And when it was dead, I cut a piece off."

Aishani laughed. "Did not."

"Did too! Norris helped me so I wouldn't mess up."

"You didn't tell us about a cousin named Norris."

"Norris works for Auntie and Brother."

Anita yawned, then put her hands behind her head. "I still don't believe you weren't scared," she said. "You can't even jump from the top of the stairs to the bottom like we do."

"Well, I wasn't scared of this."

"I'm gonna ask your mom when she comes," she said.

"Go ahead. She'll tell you I didn't scream."

Anita's mom picked her up before mine did, and I no longer had to fret so much about the possibility of exposure — I knew the other girls were less likely to press it. By the time my own mother came for me their insults didn't have such a mean bite. They didn't feel like they were meant for an outsider; there was a subtle warmth of good nature now, of the kind of inclusion I'd had and lost with my cousins.

My mother passed her tired eyes over me in the passenger's seat. Even at ten my feet didn't touch the ground. "Had a good time at Jordan's?"

"It was fun," I said. "I want to go over more, if that's okay."

"Maybe."

We had to stop for gas before going home; a wood-panelled boat of a machine, my mother's station wagon always seemed in need of gas and plagued us with new worries instead of simply ridding us of our old ones. I remembered her face when she first saw the car, how her nose wrinkled in disgust, but the woman who was selling it knocked the price down to a number my mother couldn't afford to say no to.

She stuck me in the line to pay while she went to the fridges for some milk, promising me a chocolate bar when we reached the cashier. The woman in front of me took her receipt from the cashier and headed out to her pump, and then a man cut in front of me.

"Excuse me," said my mother. She walked from the back of the store to the counter, a slim box of 2 percent in her hand. "You just cut in front of my daughter."

"Oh," the man said.

"'Oh'?" my mother repeated. "She was next in line. Go to the back."

"Jesus Christ," said the man. He was beefy and mean-looking: buzzed blond hair, a red skull-and-bones T-shirt stretched over his chest. I wanted to tell my mother to leave him alone. "I could've paid for the gas

in the amount of time you stood here bitching at me,"
he said. "What's your fucking problem?"

"That you didn't wait your turn. Get to the back of
the goddamn line."

"Mummy—"

I tugged on her jacket but she slapped my hand away
and I recoiled from the sting.

The cashier started to raise his hands in a plea for
my mother and the man to calm down, and nervous-
ness shivered through the line; the people behind us
started to fidget.

"I don't like this," I whispered. "I don't like this, I
don't like this . . ."

The man headed out of the store, pushing open the
door so that it thumped against the outer wall. "Always
something with you fucking people."

My mother slammed the milk down on the counter
and yelled the pump number to the cashier. She turned
to me. "Why were you going to tell me to stop?"

"I just didn't want to—"

"What? Want to what, Kara?"

I started to chew on my lower lip and hoped that
by some miracle the floor would open up and swallow
me whole and cushion me from her voice. "I wanted
to forget about it."

"Of course. You want to forget everything! I don't

know how you got to be so soft. Everyone will walk all over you if you just 'forget' it. Come on, let's go."

My mother banged out of the store without bothering to get a receipt, and I gave the cashier a small, apologetic smile before following her to the car.

AFTER ABOUT A week, my teachers got wind of the pig's head — probably because its severance became bloodier and more gruesome with every telling. My mother's warning about being soft bounced around in my head, and soon I started adding new embellishments to the story.

"Have you ever heard a pig scream?" I'd ask, and after seeing a bunch of brown-haired heads wag from side to side, I'd shudder. "It's really bad. I'm telling you."

Every recess and during stolen moments in class, I'd report a new detail to my adoring audience: how the pig, being so strong and fat, gave us such a hard time when we grabbed it in its pen that Norris had to bash its head in with a hammer before I cut in with the knife; how I wasn't wearing any gloves, so the blood poured warm and thick and sticky onto my hands. And then after school, when I finished my homework and I made my way down to the 7-Eleven with Rochelle and the rest of the girls (and sometimes even the boys from our block), I'd saunter down the sidewalk and sip my Slurpee and say, "Even when they skinned it, I didn't look away. Not once."

Quickly, I became one of the most popular kids in my grade. I was up there with Savannah Evans and Nicholas Lombardi. Savannah was the richest kid in school; Nick, with his long eyelashes and dirty-blond cherub curls, was the cutest; and I was suddenly the craziest. Older sisters brought their younger siblings to me to be frightened and amazed, and in the playground boys started inviting me to play Red Ass with them, whipping me with the tennis ball as hard as they whipped each other.

Popularity did not claim me in my neighbourhood like it did at school, but there, nobody felt the need to translate for me anymore, to always bring up the great misfortune of being Canadian-born. I got bored of the live pig, of describing how boldly I'd watched its slaughter, and I moved on to explaining how I'd helped Auntie prepare jerk pork out of the butchered body. After that, whoever I hung out with mentioned fruits like skinup without asking me if I knew what they were, not asking me if I even knew what the Jamaican name for them — guinep — was, and they yelled "Wah gwa'an?" when they saw me instead of "Oh, hey."

For a week I blustered around school and swaggered

down Marlee Avenue and silently waited for the attention I got to transform me into a girl who would actually have the moxie to slaughter a pig. But that courage never burned in my belly; that aggression never revealed itself in a disregard for rules or in a penchant for pranks like it did with my friends. My sense of boldness only lasted for as long as my description of the pig did.

I didn't know that the teachers had found out about my stories until a Monday afternoon when I saw my mother standing in the hallway just before final recess. We all queued up to leave and when Miss Kakos, the student teacher, opened the classroom door to let us out, I saw my mother leaning against the plastered wall, a chewed-tip pencil jutting through her messy ponytail of relaxed hair, her tattered knapsack by her feet.

The sight of her made my fingers quiver. She had no place in my stories; she didn't belong with any of the identities I constructed during the time I spent at school.

Miss Kakos shepherded the kids to the yard, and Ms. Gold put her hand on my back and beckoned for my mother to come inside. I was in a split-grade class so my classroom was one of the largest in the school, divided into sections: Reading Section, Working Section, Science Section, Cleansing Section. I'd heard my mother whisper to her other mother-friends about schools that had walls and ceilings falling apart, about schools that packed children into portables because of lack of space—but my school wasn't like that. Every room was big and colourful and chock full of brand-new equipment the school fundraised for. My classmates were picked up in Range Rovers and BMWs driven by their nannies and occasionally their parents. Sometimes the parents would stop my mother and offer her a job.

"I'm picking up my own child," she'd say before walking away.

I'd be right next to her, tugging on her sleeve. "Why did Katie's mom ask if you needed a job when you have one?"

"Stop talking, Kara," she'd whisper back, her face tight.

Ms. Gold led us to the Corrective Section, which was really just her desk. She sat down behind it and gestured for my mother and me to sit in the two blue stack chairs on the other side.

"I'm just going to get right to the point, Mrs.—I'm sorry, Miss Davis," said Ms. Gold, folding her hands together. "There has been a rumour around the school—started by Kara—that she killed a pig on your vacation to Jamaica. The children have been abuzz with it. It seems to be quite the playground story."

"You called me down here because my daughter told a lie?"

"So the story isn't true?"

"No," said my mother. "But even if it were, a child witnessing or helping out with butchering isn't unusual or uncommon in Jamaica. But no, my daughter didn't participate in either activity."

"Miss Davis, to be frank, whether or not the story is true is irrelevant. It's the nature of the lie that's concerning."

My mother looked at me, but I lowered my head so as to not meet her stare. I went over the story in my mind: the blood, the knife, the hammer, the screams. It no longer came to me in images; now it just seemed like words that didn't belong to me.

"From what Miss Kakos, Mr. Roberts — the gym teacher — and I have gathered, Kara has exhibited pleasure and enthusiasm toward the concept of slaughtering an animal."

"Well, children enthusiastically step on worms, rip the legs off a daddy-long-legs, squish bees. Kids are intrigued by the concept of death."

"I understand that this is a delicate topic, and I am not hurrying to any conclusions. However, perhaps it would be good for Kara to see the school's child psychologist —"

"Let me stop you right there," said my mother, raising her hand. She paused for a beat and then smiled the way I'd see her do sometimes when a cashier or a waiter or our landlord got on her nerves.

"Ms. Gold, did you also know that I'm quite familiar with educational protocol?" she said. "And I believe that for a situation like this, the protocol is that before prescribing the school's psychologist, the teacher must give the parent the option to take their child to a family doctor who would then offer their own referral."

Ms. Gold pressed her lips together, a flush of red colouring her neck. When my mother finished speaking, she cleared her throat. "I ultimately don't believe that the situation is all that serious," she said. "I just thought you should know."

"Thank you for your concern, and rest assured it will be dealt with. If you don't mind," said my mother, standing up. I got up with her. "I would like to take Kara home now."

In the car, my mother turned to me, her finger pointed in my face. "Do you realize what you've done?"

"Mom—"

"I'm speaking." She snapped her fingers loudly, and I flinched. "These people already look at me like I'm trash, Kara."

I opened my mouth to speak even though I had no

idea what to say her, but she just shook her head and turned away from me, resting back against her seat. "I do not need you making things worse by lying. Why would you even say that you killed a pig?"

I stayed silent, hunched in my seat; my eyes wandered as if scouting out an exit strategy, though I knew I could never just open the door and walk away from her.

My mother banged her palm against the steering wheel. "I asked you a question."

"I don't know why I did it," I said. "I'm sorry."

"You're a little liar. If you were sorry you'd just stop making up stories," she said. "I don't know what I did to make you this way. Did you tell anyone from the neighbourhood?"

I squeezed my index and middle fingers with my left hand. "Just that I saw it. But nobody cares there, and you said that in Jamaica—"

"That isn't the point," she said. "I'm dropping you off at Nana's. She's off work today. I need to go back to the library, and I just can't deal with you right now."

"We only live one street over from her. If anything happens I can call her and she can come over. Please don't make me go over there."

"You not wanting to go to Nana's just makes me want to leave you there even more. Put on your seat belt."

. . .

BEFORE MY MOTHER dropped me off at Nana's front door, she instructed me to tell my grandmother what I'd said about the pig's head.

"And I'll know if you don't," she'd said.

Telling Nana what I'd told my friends and the kids at school was easy: it was what came after that made me run into the guestroom and collapse on the bed, my face buried in one of the floral pillows that had been placed perfectly against the headboard. The door was closed, but I could hear my grandmother calling all the right people in the neighbourhood to tell them about what I'd done.

"She a bright-eye likkle pickney," she said to Rochelle's great-aunt. "I tell her say, 'Yuh make yuh sail too big fi yuh boat, yuh sail will capsize yuh!' She always make up story them, from when she was small! No way her mother let her slice up a pig, my daughter nuh crazy!"

Of course my friends' mothers told them all about it, and of course none of them was surprised. And when I ran into the group on my way to the 7-Eleven, they acted as much.

"Hey, Kara," said Jordan, sucking on a rocket popsicle.

"We were gonna see if we could get into the school and run up to the roof," said Rochelle. "Wanna come?"

"I'm okay. Thanks."

"I told you she'd say no, Chelle," said Anita, smirking as she walked past me, knocking her shoulder into mine. "She's too scared."

AFTER MY MOTHER'S visit I'd been afraid Ms. Gold would tell the class I'd been lying, but two days later I was still being asked about Hanover. I ended up repeating details rather than adding new ones; forgetting to lean in close at certain points and yell at others; not bothering to whisper to inspire shivers or to widen my eyes to elicit gasps. At recess, I leaned against the trunk of the giant willow tree that sprouted from a patch of dirt dug into the pavement, watching some boys play Cops and Robbers while a group of girls played Mail Man, Mail Man, their legs stretched painfully wide in near-splits. After a few minutes, I saw Anna Mae walking up to me, her French braids tied together with a lavender ribbon that criss-crossed in and out. She leaned next to me.

"I never see you alone," she said.

Her voice was softer than I'd expected. Too soft for a kitten-killer.

"Just feel like sitting out."

"You're standing."

"Yeah," I said.

"Yeah," she said.

We stood together for a while in a silence that I found unusual but not uncomfortable. It even felt peaceful. It was a silence that gave me the opportunity to settle into myself, to hear myself breathe and think.

I looked at Anna Mae in her purple corduroy overalls and noticed for the first time that her skin was a sort of greyish-cream and that her eyes were green. She pushed her hands deep into her pockets and slowly raised her head so that the back of it rested against the trunk and some of the bark chipped off into her hair. I felt no desire to think of a crazy anecdote for her to listen to, no need to twist myself into a new identity. I just felt like talking to her.

"It must've sucked watching kittens die."

"I was six the first time. I threw up," she said.

I stood there and imagined what it would be like to watch a kitten, barely bigger than a grown-up's hand, get dunked and held under water.

"I didn't do it, you know," I said. "Kill a pig? Made it all up."

She smiled. "That's okay."

"Yeah?"

"Yeah."

The bell rang, and I could hear the collective groan

of kids mid-game — they'd have to wait till lunchtime to pick up where they'd left off, and there'd no doubt be shouts for do-overs and clean slates. Anna Mae and I walked quietly together to the nearest school doors, side-stepping a tennis ball rolling its way down to the fences, completely abandoned by the boys who'd been playing Red Ass ten minutes earlier.

SNOW DAY

AT THE END OF THIRD PERIOD JUST BEFORE lunch, Principal Carrington declared the afternoon a snow day and told us all to go home. Outside, the streets were dusted like powdered sugar and the snowbanks around the sidewalks were tiny white-and-grey mounds that reached only as high as my ankles, but we were told that a little after midday, easterly winds would be blowing through the city. We were told that the gusts would threaten to rip trees out from the concrete, and would bring with them the type of snow you wish for at Christmas. The type of snow that whites out the blueness of the sky; that forces cars to crawl inch by inch on the highway because whiteness is all anyone can see. And Principal Carrington was kicking us out before we could be trapped inside to wreak havoc on her school.

"Aww yeah!" My class started to howl. Even I joined the others when they banged their fists on the desks. I was in Extended French, and all of my classes today were with Mme. Rizzoli. I would've wished for an earthquake to get out of spending even one more minute trying to translate my thoughts into another language.

"SNOW DAY! SNOW DAY! SNOW DAY!" we chanted.

"*Taisez-vous!*" Mme. Rizzoli snapped, putting her hands on her hips. "You are all eighth-graders, act like it!"

We pressed our smiling lips together and our shoulders shook with silent laughter. "Snow day. Snow day. Snow day," we whispered.

"*J'ai dit taisez-vous!*"

Principal Carrington was still talking, her voice garbled by the PA system. "Those of you who have younger siblings in the school and those of you whose parents checked off 'Stay at school in the event of a weather emergency,' please report to the office. The rest of you get home safely."

Mme. Rizzoli turned away from the PA and faced the front of the room. "Okay—everyone walk, I repeat, *walk* to your lockers and collect your things. *À demain.*"

"*À demain*," we repeated.

The entire class ran, rushing to the door all at once, ramming against each other, trying to be the first ones to spill out into the hallway. I waited at my desk for the crowd to thin out so I could leave at my own pace without pushing against anyone: I had nowhere to hurry to. Rochelle joined me as I headed out of the classroom and told me all of our friends were going to hang out at her place for the rest of the day. Was I coming?

"I can't. My mom checked off the box," I said.

"So? Just leave. You know these white-bread teachers don't give a shit about what we do."

The rest of our friends — Anita, Jordan, and Aishani — were at their lockers packing their things. Anita came over to us, twirling her straightened hair into a ponytail high up on her head.

"Nuh fret it, Chelle, you know she's not gonna come. She too 'fraid of Mummy. Got her on lockdown and shit, she canna even run 'cross di street fi buy a patty at lunch."

"Kara, I live two streets over from you," Rochelle said. "Just come."

I had never been to Rochelle's house when her mother wasn't around, and never for more than a couple of hours: my mother always called me home way before the other girls had to leave. And every time I was forced to leave, something good would happen: Truth or Dare or a scary movie on TV or a game of Nicky Nicky Nine Doors. The next day they'd all laugh about a moment I'd missed. I'd smile with them and then they would look at me, all of their eyebrows raised. "What're you laughing at? You weren't even there." They would continue to giggle, and I would bite my lip and watch. To stay in the group, thick skin was a must—being able to take an insult was respected just as much as being able to throw shade.

Aishani and Jordan tilted their heads up in my direction. "So what's going on, Kara?" they asked. "You coming?"

"Just come," said Rochelle. "You never do anything."

There were no adults in the hallway to see me leave and Rochelle was right: the teachers here really didn't care about you if you weren't a student in their class anyway. It wasn't like my old school downtown on Ferndale Avenue, where everything and everyone was under watch. I'd had to beg my mother to transfer me out and away from those kids who were so eager to comment on my thick lips and grab fistfuls of my kinky hair; beg her to let me do my two years of junior high around the neighbourhood, around my friends from the block.

"If you get into any sort of trouble, I will pull you out

and enroll you back downtown, you understand me?" she'd said. "That includes failing math."

"Yes, Mummy."

I looked back toward the stairs that led up to the office, rubbing my palm against the back of my neck.

"I told you she'd stay," said Anita, smirking.

For once, I wanted to shock that smirk off her face. I turned to her. "Fuck it," I said. "Let's go."

Anita narrowed her eyes as I opened my locker and started packing my things. Everyone had left the hallway except us. Rochelle and the rest were grouped together in a circle, wearing cropped winter jackets with fur-trimmed hoods, their hair freshly relaxed or pulled back into ringletted ponytails, their tight jeans tucked into suede boots that reached their knees. I didn't look as good in my clothes as they did in theirs. I had no meat on my bones, no pout to my lips, and they were all starting to curve into that thickness Island boys loved, their eyebrows cocked in that flirty curiosity that got those boys' attention.

"They're faas," my mother would say, "and one of them is going to end up pregnant. Just watch."

Behind me, Jordan and Aishani were arguing over just how cute Jhamar, the student council president, was, Aishani rolling the *R*'s with her tongue every time. She was Indian, like from India Indian, but told any boy who swaggered up to her that she was Trini and explained that being born in Canada meant she couldn't put on the accent. Once we asked her what the capital of Trinidad was. When she said Tobago we doubled over laughing, and later on that day she pulled me to the side to ask what was so funny about her answer.

I zipped up my jacket and swung my knapsack over my shoulder.

"Ay, look at this, Kara ah take charge! She think she a bad gyal for she break the rules dey," said Jordan, laughing with Rochelle.

"She'll probably cave halfway to your house and run back to school, Chelle."

"Quiet, Anita. Yuh run yuh mouth too much," I said.

"What's this? Miss Canada gwine fi bust out the patois? Yuh need to stop Ja-fakin' it, Kara."

I opened my mouth to respond but felt my shoulders roll back, felt acrid spit fill my mouth, and knew I looked the way the women in my family did when they had a loud point to make. Trouble usually followed whenever they spoke in that stance, and I wasn't up for that. I kept walking. I always lost when I went head-to-head with Anita anyway; her comebacks were harsher and her accent was better. Real. Not something she had to put on. The rest of us just cobbled together what we could from listening to our parents or grandparents, but

Anita was fresh from Jamaica — there was no competing, especially when I had the weakest accent out of all the Canadian-borns.

We pushed through the doors and stepped out into the schoolyard. The snow had started to fall, light and fast and fluffy; it was good for packing, for snowmen and snowballs, but I wasn't fooled. This was how all storms started. Gently.

We all tugged our hoods over our heads, Rochelle and Anita squealing every time the snow dappled their straightened strands with wetness. Already, I could see the frizz coming out, kinky and tight, disrupting the silkiness they'd endured the hot comb for the night before. I grazed my palm over my scalp to see if my braids were still smooth. They weren't, but it could've been worse.

Our school was right at Vaughan and Oakwood, hidden in one of the residential pockets in the centre of the area where the Caribbean and Europe converged. Once you left the playground you could turn right toward downtown and head to Little Italy on St. Clair West; but we were turning left up toward Eglinton West and Marlee: Island Town. The walk in either direction was mixed with both groups, though. Bungalow windows boasted the colourful banners of the Island flags: red, yellow, and green for Guyana; black, yellow, and green for Jamaica. Nonnas and nonnos crowded every other porch, teetering on rocking chairs, drinking beer or Brio Chinotto, their pit bulls snarling in the backyard.

"I can't get my hood to stay on," said Jordan, bunching up her jacket at the neck so that the snow wouldn't get through the gap and melt on her chest.

"White girls can get their hair wet," said Rochelle. "Stop frontin' like you need your hood."

The rest of us laughed, and Jordan gave us the finger. She was mixed. Her mother was black Guyanese and her father was Canadian. Seventh-generation Canadian, too, not Italian-Canadian or Portuguese or anything. She'd come out a light, light milky brown — almost beige — with a small pointed nose, hazel eyes, and hair that was short and auburn and kind of curly but mostly straight. The year before, she'd done a home spray tan to make herself darker but ended up making herself orange instead. I was the only one who knew that. I don't know if it was because I didn't go to school with everyone yet or because she knew I was too nice to say anything to anyone, but she'd told the others she couldn't go to school because of the flu.

The snow was up to our shins now and the wind had started slanting its fall, blowing it in our direction so that snowflakes pelted into our eyes and stuck our eyelashes together. I nuzzled my nose against my scarf and trudged forward. Some of the boys in our grade had decided to stay in the playground, whipping snowballs at each other, their screams and laughter too stubborn to be drowned out by the wind.

"Let's get fries from New Orleans Donuts," said Aishani. "I'm starving."

"It's too cold to walk around. We can order pizza at my place," said Rochelle.

"With what money? You've got, like, two dollars to your name," said Jordan.

"That's two dollars more than you. And anyway, my mom left me money for an emergency. We're good."

"But I feel for fries," said Aishani.

No one had said anything about stopping anywhere. I turned to them but tried to keep my face buried in my hood—more as a way to hide my panicked expression than to shield myself from the cold. "Can't we just go to Chelle's house? That's what we said we'd do."

"If you're going to be this way, you should just go back to school," said Anita.

"Well, I actually don't care where we go," said Rochelle, "as long as we go Vaughan way."

"What's so special about Vaughan way?" said Jordan. "You always want to walk that way."

"I just like it," said Rochelle.

"Yeah, but why?"

The high school was on Vaughan Road, and Rochelle was seeing a guy who went there: Chris Richardson, grade ten. Every girl knew Chris; every mother, too. He never kept himself out of trouble: trespassing, tagging buildings, mouthing off to cops who spot-checked him and his crew at the park or in front of the McDonald's or by the bus stop. But he was always quick to carry your mother's grocery bags to the door or help your grandmother find a seat in church, and he did it all with sly silences and toothy smiles and, if you were lucky, a wink behind your mother's back.

"Be careful of boys like him," they'd tell us. "Yuh need fi stay clear from bright-eye boys like that."

"Your dad was like that," my mother would add. "And look how I turned out."

The day Chris and Rochelle first said "hey" to each other, we were at Vaughan Road Academy for a tour, trying to see if that was the school we wanted to spend the next four years at, me pretending like I had a say in where I ended up. He'd stopped her in the hallway, took her by the hand and guided her to him, putting his hands around her waist as she stood in the space between his spread-out legs; it was a move she was used to. Rochelle had that really fair rose-brown complexion, that kind of red skin and shapely heaviness that made cars slow down and girls up-down, and she'd been dealing with hungry-eyed boys since she was ten.

While they were talking I'd pretended to flip through the notes my mother had told me to write down, far enough behind Rochelle that I wasn't interrupting but close enough that if she wanted out she could just turn to me and we'd walk away together, our arms linked. Chris had thought she was a transfer student, a sophomore like him, and only when he took down her number did Rochelle tell him she'd just turned fourteen and was in grade eight. First he got quiet. Then he left without even saying bye. But later on that night, she called me and said that he'd rung her up and they'd just finished a three-hour conversation.

"Just don't tell anyone," she'd said. "It's a secret, okay?"

Sometimes we both pictured the licks she'd get if her mom ever found out about Chris—and Rochelle's mom didn't play around: she used the belt. My mother didn't like to use objects; she always said her hands were sharp enough. I tried to imagine keeping something like a boy from her—if a boy ever showed any interest in me—and I felt my body turn in on itself. Even the backs of my eyeballs throbbed as if they'd grown strained from searching for her open-palmed hand. It was how I felt when I let myself think that a storefront boy might be smirking at me; a panic would creep up on my body like a slow-moving fever and then for a brief moment I'd feel glad that I wasn't sexy enough to keep a secret like Rochelle's.

WE CROSSED THE street to New Orleans Donuts and stumbled over ourselves to get inside and out of the snow. The warmth of the shop was heavy with the smell of frying batter and loud with the sounds of chatter mixed with the *pew pews* of the two arcade games by the washroom. It was packed. Each of the four corner tables had been seized by a school, from high-school kids from Vaughan Road Academy (they took up two tables) to other students from our school to the kids from St. Thomas Aquinas, another Catholic school just up the street from ours.

Rochelle scanned the store, her eyes slowly sweeping over the boys in oversized coats and fur trapper hats. When she found Chris over by the window, in the corner across from the entrance, sprawled out and laughing with three of his friends, she took off her hood, shook her hair back and looked the other way in a display of nonchalance. I was the only one who noticed the move and I couldn't tell if her plan was working.

Chris was focused on his friends still, all of them

bumping fists and shoving shoulders and shouting, "That's respect, man. That's respect!" but his attention seemed to have shifted somehow; even though he never looked away from his group, it was like he knew ours had arrived. But maybe he did that with all the girls; maybe he was just weighing his options. His friends appeared oblivious. I recognized all three of them; they didn't have reputations like Chris's, but they were the boys you went after if Chris wasn't into you. They were the boys Anita, Aishani, and Jordan got.

Aishani bought a large poutine and found us a deserted table in the middle of the store. We all started digging in with our plastic forks, the fries nice and crunchy beneath the hot gravy and melting cheese curds.

"I'm just saying," said Jordan, "I find snow romantic."

"What's romantic about this? We're in a fucking storm."

"I'm with Anita on this one," said Aishani. "Nothing romantic about freezing your ass off."

"Well obviously not this kind of snow. Like the snow in that movie. You know, the one with that white dude."

"Oh yeah. The movie with that white dude."

"You guys know what I'm talking about. They meet at a store and spend an amazing night together or whatever, but she's white-girl flaky so she writes her number in a book that's going to be sold the next day and, like, five years later, he's still trying to find that number? Searching in bookstores and shit? Chelle, you were with me when I saw it with Jackie."

I knew what movie she was talking about. I'd seen it twice. But I joined in with the others and stared at her blankly.

"Anyway, they finally meet at an ice rink and it's snowing and they make out in the snow. You wouldn't want that? I would. And if not snow then rain."

"We can't do snow or rain—think about your hair." I took off my hood and rubbed the top of my head. "Look at Chelle." Everyone turned to Rochelle, whose hair was now in that stage between natural and straightened. Puffs of tangled curls spiralled out from behind her ears while the part of her hair that was still straight lay flat atop the kinks, giving her a bizarre mushroom head. "She looks like a palm tree."

"Fuck off," said Rochelle, but then she touched the back of her head and glanced in Chris's direction. "Wait, do I really, though?"

Anita nodded and Rochelle rushed to the washroom. I took another forkful of poutine and smiled at the gentle embarrassment I'd caused; no real harm was done, but the insult was enough to make Jordan snigger appreciatively, which earned me points.

No one said anything for a bit, each of us focusing on our forks, fighting each other for more cheese on our fries.

Then Aishani spoke. "Kara, I think Chris is looking at you."

"And his boy Devon," said Jordan.

I tried to keep my eyes from widening with alarm. "What?"

"Yeah, he's been staring at you since we came in," said Aishani.

"Maybe he's just checkin' for Chelle," I said. "They always check for her."

Rochelle returned to the table, her hair in a high ponytail with a thin black headband around her edges to hide the frizz. "What's going on?"

"Chris and Devon are checking Kara out," said Jordan.

"I don't know what they're talking about," I said quickly. Too quickly.

Rochelle turned around and after a few seconds she looked back at me and giggled. "They're checking you out for sure. You got eyes in your head?"

I didn't know what to do. I looked at Rochelle for some sort of sign, some kind of wordless communication to signal how I was supposed to react in this situation, but she didn't give me anything.

"*Rhatid!* Devon is smiling at you. Smile back, Kara," said Jordan. "Or wave or something. He's looking at you."

"No he's not," I said again.

Anita spoke this time. "Well he won't be checkin' for you when you look so tore-up tore-up."

"True," said Rochelle. "Go to the bathroom. Pat down your braids, put on some makeup or something for once." She rooted around in her knapsack and took out the makeup bag she hid from her mother. It was a slim case, pink and white with wide-petalled flower designs all over. She handed it to me. "Gwa'an, nuh."

"I don't know…"

They all shouted at me. "Gwa'an, nuh!"

The bathroom was small and kind of grimy. It only had two grey-doored stalls, and the white ceramic tile was yellowed and dirt-grubbed. The mirror above the sink was foggy, almost opaque; I could barely see my reflection much less use it as a guide to put on makeup. I was about to go back to the table when the door swung open and Devon walked in.

He was short for a guy but a good few inches taller than me. He had mahogany skin and a smooth, oval face, eyelashes longer than most girls', and really broad shoulders; he could probably carry me around on his back. I thought about what my mother would say if she were standing where I was, how she'd raise her head and set her jaw, how her voice would echo around the room. But all I could say was, "You know this is the girls' washroom, right?"

He smiled at me a little. "Your friends told me you were waiting for me in here."

"What? No."

"Your girl Rochelle said for me to come in here."

I waited for him to say something else but he didn't. There was only one door and he was standing right by it. I couldn't imagine Rochelle telling him that, setting me up like that. I couldn't even imagine Anita doing it. Our group could be hurtful but never cruel. Devon had to have come in on his own.

I headed toward the exit, but he shifted his weight so that he was in front of the door.

"I want to leave." I hoped my voice sounded forceful enough.

"Why?" His tone was light, like he and I were playing a game. A sick, nerve-wracking game.

"Don't be scared," he said. I *was* scared, but I didn't want him to know that. I wanted him to think I could hold my own. I wanted them all to think that.

He took a step closer to me. I took a step back. That made him chuckle and he leaned back against one of the stalls.

"Chris told me you were shy. I get it, let's just go slow."

"Chris doesn't know anything about me."

"He said you were the quiet one. Always chillin' behind your girls. C'mon, don't be so scared," he said again.

Rushing toward the door crossed my mind, but if Devon managed to block me from leaving that would just make everything worse. I took a step forward, and he pushed off from the stall.

"My food is getting cold."

He was only a foot or so away from me now.

"I bought it with the last of my allowance . . ."

"I'll get you another one after." He closed in on me, reaching up with his left hand, and pushed one of my braids off my face, his thumb brushing my cheek. My skin burned.

"I want to go." I said it again.

"Don't be like that."

His thumb was under my chin, gently tilting it upward. I turned my head away.

"Kara—"

I flinched at hearing him say my name and almost screamed when the door opened again. Devon looked behind him to see who'd come in, and I moved quickly past the girl at the door and hurried back to our table.

The chairs were empty, pushed out from the table; crumpled, gravy-stained napkins and empty Styrofoam containers littered the tabletop. I looked around but I couldn't find Rochelle and the others anywhere in the store, and white was all I could see out the windows. Blue squiggles were on one of the napkins and I picked it up.

Sorry. Jordan's handwriting.

I stared at it. They'd really left me. Devon sauntered back over to his corner, the swag in his step telling me that a lie had been whispered, that the girl from the washroom now had gossip to spread. I wasn't so *quiet* anymore and everyone would know. Laughter boomed out from the corner. Devon's friends were eyeing me and giving him props, nodding their heads in my direction. Only Chris seemed to be straight-faced and uninterested.

"Just chill, Devon," I heard him say.

"What's up with you?"

"Just calm yourself."

The loud chatter in the store trailed into mutters, and I could feel everyone glancing at me. There was no one here to have my back. The way Devon had come on, forceful without force, the stories I knew he was telling his friends, embarrassed me in a way my mother and grandmother had prepared me for. But the loneliness that empty table made me feel was new and unexpected in a way that made it hard to breathe.

I ran out into the snow, not bothering to cover my hair or button my coat. I didn't even know where I was going or where the parking lot ended and the street began. I couldn't see if there were any cars on the road or if there was anyone else walking. I wasn't even supposed to be out here.

"Ay!" a voice called. "Ay yo!"

I ignored it and lowered my head to my chest to keep my face from the cutting snow, making sure I only stepped in the footholes made from people who'd managed through earlier. There was a small black glove on the ground, and I hoped it belonged to Rochelle or Jordan or anyone from the group and that her hand was a rainbow of white, blue, and purple. I hoped they were all freezing, that little icicles were forming on their eyelashes and making them stick together. I hoped, prayed, that their hair would give way to the wetness and tangle in on itself, knotting and coiling, shrinking and puffing so that they'd cry out when their mothers combed through it before they went to bed. And I wouldn't be there to listen to them whisper sheepishly about how they'd bawled and screamed for respite from the pain. I wouldn't be there to listen to them whisper about anything anymore.

"Ay!"

A hand touched my shoulder and I whirled around. The person took a step back. It was Chris. "Sorry — you weren't turning around. It's freezing out here. I can't see shit."

"What do you want?"

"To give you a ride. I have my brother's car today."

"No." I started walking again. He kept pace beside me, trudging through fresh snow.

"Why? I just want to give you a ride."

We were nearing what I thought was the sidewalk and I stopped walking, trying to reach a decision about where I wanted to go. Rochelle's house was on Hopewell Avenue — not too far. If I followed them there they'd know I could take whatever they threw at me and if I didn't they'd write me off as sensitive, the worst thing you could be in that group, in this neighbourhood.

"Listen," said Chris. "What Devon did was foul. I know that."

"If you know, who're you going to tell?"

He paused and then sighed, silently admitting to what I already knew: boys didn't rat on each other even if they were in the wrong, *especially* if they were in the wrong.

"Your girls snaked you. Devon snaked you. Just let me give you a ride. I won't do anything. My car is right there." He pointed to what looked like an old Honda parked in front of New Orleans Donuts.

The wind howled, and I shivered in my jacket. "Whatever."

We didn't speak on the way over to his car and once we were inside, he cranked the heat up to full blast and turned on the radio so that 50 Cent's beat bumped in the car. I cupped my hands around my mouth and breathed on them, rubbing my palms together. Going to Rochelle's seemed like the expected thing to do, almost like a natural choice, but something that felt like doubt hollowed out my stomach; joining them might prove I could shake off humiliation, but it would also prove that there were no limits to the kind of humiliation they could put me through.

Chris backed out slowly and told me he had to put his hand on the back of my headrest so he could see better. It wasn't until we were already on the road that I began to wonder if anyone had seen me get in, if there was even just one person who'd been able to make me out through the snow.

"Where should I take you?"

The heat from the car started steaming up the windows and my eye followed a water droplet streak down the glass. I thought about my grandmother and how when I was a child and a creak in the house or a squeak of a chair made me flinch she'd say, "Duppy know who fi frighten." The first time she said it I asked her what it meant, and she only told me that I had to learn to steel myself so I wouldn't be a target for any ghost; so spirit and human would know better than to target me and would know to leave me alone.

"Kara," said Chris. "Where do you want to go?"

I faced front and put my hands to my mouth again. "Just take me back to school," I said.

BEFORE/AFTER

ON THURSDAY AFTERNOON, MR. ESPOSITO TOLD Anita and me that we had to go down to the cafeteria.

"Why us?" said Anita.

"Both of you are going to the Sharing Circle this afternoon, aren't you? It's in the cafeteria. Put your books in your lockers."

When we made it out into the hallway, Anita banged her locker open and slammed it shut. I could hear her muttering to herself.

"Why he gotta tell the world my business like that."

I spoke beneath my breath. "Everyone would've seen us leave anyway."

Anita turned to me. "Who asked you?"

I closed my locker and walked down the hall without saying anything back. Anita was always too quick to start an argument, and I didn't want to have one right where Mr. Esposito could hear us. But the anticipation of a fight didn't scare me like it usually did. It had been two weeks since I'd spoken to her or any of our other friends, two weeks since they abandoned me at New Orleans Donuts. And every day for those two weeks, something inside of me had been ready for a confrontation.

She did have a point about the Sharing Circle, though. If Anita, Rochelle, Jordan, and I had all gone together, like I'd planned, we would've been protected by our numbers. The other kids would know that it was a con, a Get Out of Jail Free card. But with just two of us going, it looked like we had issues we were desperate to share. Issues that could be used against us, that could be used as ammunition.

We'd first heard about the Sharing Circle the morning before the snow day — though Mme. Rizzoli had nearly forgotten to tell us. When the morning announcements were finished, we'd sat at our desks and opened our *orthographe* Duo-Tangs without a word. In the silence, we heard Mr. Esposito tell the grade sevens about it in the adjoined room, stressing its significance, and Madame groaned at his muffled voice. She pulled a sheet of purple paper from her giant binder and held it up for us to see. The WordArt that spelled TALKING IS SHARING, SHARING IS HEALING made me fold my arms across my chest. It reminded me of the pamphlets I always saw people handing out at St. George subway station or outside the Eaton Centre, the pamphlets my mother said cults used to lure the weak-minded. After holding the paper up for a few seconds, Madame flipped it back around. She recited the most basic details in English and then started adding things in French, speaking swiftly as if she couldn't wait to spit the words out of her mouth.

"Aucun de vous n'êtes obliger d'assister cela, mais c'est encouragée. C'est un espace sûr pour chacun d'entre vous de parler."

This had been when Rochelle and I still sat next to each other in the fourth row, and she'd nudged me with her elbow. "She's talking way too fast. What's she saying?"

Anita and Aishani sat behind us and they inched forward to hear my translation. I tried to keep my voice as low as possible; I'd already gotten detention for speaking out of turn, and Madame had threatened to call home if it happened again.

"We don't have to go if we don't want to," I whispered, "but they think it's a good idea."

"How is talking to a room full of strangers about my problems a good idea? So fool-fool."

"Anita, you *need* an entire room of people to work out all the issues you got."

"That's cute, Shani, what's the capital of Trinidad again?"

Rochelle snorted in laughter and I nudged her. "Shut up," I muttered.

"Kara!" Mme. Rizzoli's voice made me look up to the chalkboard at the front of the room. "Detention," she said.

"But Madame, I —"

I'd spoken in English, which automatically stripped me of morning recess on top of my after-school detention. I kept quiet to avoid more strikes even though I could hear Anita and Aishani sniggering behind me, even though they both kept poking me hard in the back, increasing my frustration with every jab, willing me, tempting me to turn around and snap at them so I could get into even more trouble.

At three thirty that day, five other students had dragged their feet to Madame's room to serve their punishment. A seventh-grader, Manuela Lao, and her friend Cristina sat next to each other and whispered about the Sharing Circle, about how going to the session would mean getting out of class all Thursday afternoon. It was how I got the idea: if I told the others about the chance to miss class, it would earn me, at bare minimum, a week of amnesty — for a while, at least, I'd be off-limits when they threw shots at each other. And not because they thought I was too soft to handle the teasing, either, but because I'd earned it. That amnesty probably would've saved me from being snaked at New Orleans Donuts two weeks ago.

When Madame dismissed us at half past four, I told her I wanted to put my name down on the sign-up sheet for the circle. Her beady blue eyes surveyed me.

"It's not like you pay attention in class anyway. I'll let Mr. Esposito know that you're signing up."

BY THE TIME Anita and I reached the cafeteria, there were about ten other students milling around the entrance. The long rectangular tables that normally crowded the room were folded and pressed against the far wall and there was a bohemian rug in the middle of the floor with fourteen tasselled cushions surrounding it. Two people were already sitting, cross-legged: one was a blond man in cargo pants and a wool cardigan over a purple dashiki; the other was a skinny brown-haired woman in a smiley-face sweater.

Mr. Silva, the gym teacher, was sitting on a stacking

chair in the far corner, reading a newspaper. I groaned softly. I hated him. Hated the way he was always dressed in all blue, from his Maple Leafs cap to his windbreaker pants. Hated how his breath always smelled of coffee. But mostly I hated the way he hated us—not all of us, just some of us. He was the kind of teacher who made me wonder why he became a teacher at all, since most kids only seemed to anger him.

"Please join us!" said the woman. "Come in; don't be shy."

The other students walked farther into the cafeteria and started to sit down. Anita and I found cushions on opposite sides of the circle.

"Hi, guys! My name is Liz and this is my co-partner Jason. I'm going to be totally upfront with you: this is my first day on the job. Jason's been around the block a few more times than I have, so I'm sorry if I seem a little nervous."

She smiled around at us, and I wasn't sure if she wanted to comfort us or be comforted by us, but we all simply stared back at her.

"Right," she said. "So before we really get into it, we'll do something super-easy, like telling everyone in the circle our names."

"We all already know each other," said Anita. "And you just told us who you were." Her tone was blunt and unforgiving. I had to appreciate it even though it killed me to.

"Doesn't matter. It's just to break the ice," she said. "Hi, my name is Liz." She turned to Jason, who told us his name for a second time.

Everyone went around introducing themselves like how they do in the AA meetings held in the basement of my grandmother's church. I'd witnessed the beginning of one of those meetings two years ago when I was eleven, when I helped Nana deliver some of her fried dumplings for Tuesday Evening Bible Study and mistook the meeting for the class. Nana had found me and ushered me back up the stairs.

"The people them sick," she'd told me.

"They don't look sick," I said. "Maybe a little tired."

"Sick in the spirit," she clarified. "They must gather together and talk fi rid themselves of what troubles them, of what turn them over to vice."

"Should we do that then?" I'd asked her.

She looked at me. "We strong. There's no need fi talk."

When the last person said their name (Jamal), Liz's face flushed red with accomplishment. "That was great!" she said.

We said nothing back.

She glanced at Jason, who nodded at her, encouraging

her to keep speaking. "So, how many of you are here because you signed up?" she asked.

I looked around the circle. About five kids had their hands half-raised. Liz nodded. "And how many of you are here because a teacher thought this would be a helpful way for you to communicate?"

The rest of the students raised their hands, including Anita. I pressed my lips together to keep from smirking and saw her narrowing her eyes at me from across the circle.

"And what about you?"

It was Jason who'd spoken this time. He turned to me and all of the other students looked in my direction, their blank eyes pressuring me for a response.

"What?—I mean, excuse me?"

"You didn't raise your hand either time," he said.

"I wasn't told to come here by a teacher . . ."

"So you signed up?"

Anita raised her eyebrows and whispered loudly. "Some people have no shame and like to talk-talk their business."

My stomach dropped and I made sure what I said next came out clearly.

"I did sign up but not because I wanted to be here. I just didn't want to be in math class."

Liz squirmed on her cushion but Jason nodded. "I

like your honesty." He addressed the entire circle. "And guys, we don't take it personally if you think this circle is complete B.S., you know, because most kids do. I would too if I were your age. But who knows, what you share here could end up surprising you."

I didn't look at him as he spoke but fixed my eyes on the dashiki he wore. I wondered if there was a tag sewn into the back and hoped that it itched his skin if there was. It was only after my palms started to hurt that I took my eyes off the deep purple — Barney purple — of his tunic and realized that my hands were clenched, my nails digging into my skin. Jason glanced at my hands and then looked at me with something like understanding or sympathy, but that only made my palms curl into fists again.

He continued to speak to everyone in the cafeteria. "I don't want anyone here to be uncomfortable," he said. "This is what we call a safe space, which means that we're all free to talk here because nothing we say will leave this circle, all right?"

Liz looked around to make sure we all at least nodded or sing-songed half-hearted yeses. When she was satisfied she smiled again and I rolled my eyes. Nothing about her or Jason made me want to stay here, but the liberation from class kept me cross-legged on the floor.

"I think we're ready to really get started. It's okay to still be a little shy, but I think we can delve right in."

Liz reached beside her into a tote bag with a green tree on the front, the words ECO-FRIENDLY stamped beneath the trunk. She pulled out a short wooden stick decorated with different-coloured feathers and dangling beads and then held it out for all of us to see.

"This is called a Talking Stick," she said. "Many Indigenous tribes use it in councils. They pass it around a circle, and only the person who is in possession of the stick gets to speak. Everyone else has to listen. We're going to use it today, but if you don't want to say anything then you can just pass the stick to the person next to you, okay?" She turned to Jamal, who was sitting on her left. "So, the first question I'll pose to the circle is, What are your biggest fears? Jamal, you can start us off."

She gave him the stick and he immediately passed it to the person beside him, who handed it off to the girl next to her.

Jason watched the Talking Stick get transferred from student to student without pause. "Guys, remember, this is a safe space . . ."

It was stupid of them to think that mattered, to think that something like that existed simply because they said it did. Jason looked behind him to Mr. Silva.

"Joe, do you have any suggestions?"

Mr. Silva shook his head without looking up from the paper.

The Talking Stick reached me and I stared at it before taking it in my hands. I expected it to feel like bark but the wood was fake to the touch. I looked at it more closely and saw that a good chunk of the coloured beads were turning silver, like any jewellery from the dollar store. It made the entire exercise feel cheap, an intimation of something that Jason and Liz didn't really get, the way they just didn't get us, and suddenly sitting through class didn't seem so bad.

"You've been holding the stick for a while, Kara. Do you want to say something?" said Jason. "It's great if you do. Come on everyone, give Kara your support."

No one in the circle did or said anything to reassure me that I'd be safe with them if I exposed myself. But I didn't expect them to. I'd never expected much from people — but what little I did I'd learned to let go of two weeks before at New Orleans Donuts. I glanced at Anita, at her round face and two afro puffs that looked like Mickey Mouse ears. Chris had told me it was Rochelle's idea to send Devon into the washroom after me, but I knew in my bones that it had been Anita's idea to abandon me at the store. She hadn't even wanted me to go with them in the first place.

I must've been looking at Anita for a while because

Jason looked from me to her and back again. "If you'd like to address someone in the circle we can allow for that," he said.

Liz looked alarmed by the idea and leaned toward Jason—but her whisper wasn't as quiet as she clearly thought it was. "Isn't that going off-script?"

"The script isn't everything," he whispered back. "It doesn't account for real-world experiences."

"But —"

"When you do this job, you're going to have to learn to adapt. Run with it."

She paused for a minute and then clapped her hands together. "Okay!" Her voice returned to that cheeriness that grated my ears. "Addressing someone in the circle is perfectly acceptable—just do so respectfully."

Anita snorted. It was a dare. I cut my eye toward her.

"There's no one in this circle *worth* addressing," I said. "Not one person."

"Kara, that's a little —"

Anita started. "Why are you looking at me for? You saying I'm wutless?"

I shrugged my shoulders. "I didn't say anything."

"Then stop looking at me when you run your mouth," said Anita.

"It's a free country. I can look at whoever the hell I want."

Liz and Jason yelled at the same time. *"Language!"*

The entire circle shivered with excitement. I could see the vicious hope in their faces, the hope that maybe this afternoon wouldn't be so boring.

Liz sputtered. "Okay, guys, I think it's time —"

"You think you're so smart, don't you?" said Anita. "Don't think I don't know what you're doing when you stay looking at me."

"I think this is what people call 'paranoid,'" I said. "Shani was right—you do have 'nuff problems. Maybe you really *do* need this circle. The teachers them think so."

"At least I didn't sign up myself."

"I signed up to get out of class. You were told to come here because you've got issues. Everyone here *knows* you've got issues—probably why you're failing, like, three classes."

There were small bursts of laughter from both sides of the circle, and Anita looked around to see who was giggling at her. Beside me, Manuela leaned to her right to talk to Cristina and she covered her mouth with her hand. "It's true, though," I could hear her say "She got an *R* in English on her report card."

Cristina laughed. "Is she so dumb that they had to make a grade just for her?" Her fake-whisper was loud enough for everyone to hear.

"Guys, safe space —"

"I wouldn't be surprised," I said loudly.

"At least I didn't go down on a dude in the girls' bathroom!"

"Only because everyone knows it's the boys' washroom you like to use!"

There was a collective "ooh" from the circle, which made me breathe easier. It gutted me, hearing her use her prank against me, knowing full well that nothing happened in that washroom, but denial only made rumours stick in this school. The best thing to do was to bury your rumour with another one.

Quickly, Anita unfolded her legs and took a step toward me — and when she moved to take another one, Mr. Silva's voice filled the cafeteria, gruff and raspy.

"Anita, that's detention!" He was no longer looking at the newspaper. "One more step and I'll send you to Principal Carrington's office and it'll be another suspension."

She hesitated, narrowing her eyes as if calculating whether or not the trouble she'd get in was worth it.

"That will be ten suspensions in two months," said Mr. Silva. "I'm not bluffing."

He wasn't. Mr. Silva loved to put us in detention or complain about us to Principal Carrington, calling us "disruptive" for lingering in the hallways, "threatening" if we were sore losers in gym class and chucked the ball against the wall if we lost King's Court. He'd sent half the kids in the circle to the office for much less.

Anita kissed her teeth and threw her hands up in the air. "This whole thing is a fucking waste anyway."

She walked toward the cafeteria doors.

"Wait," said Liz, standing up. "Where are you going?"

"*Class!*"

I watched Anita leave. It was the first time I'd ever won a round with her and the triumph made my hands and legs tremor, made my gut writhe with the urge to vomit.

"If you're not at detention by three fifteen, I'll tack on two more!" said Mr. Silva.

Anita didn't look back to acknowledge that she'd heard him.

Jason cleared his throat. "Do you want to make sure she gets to class or . . . ?"

"Why even bother," said Mr. Silva.

"Okay then," said Jason. "Maybe we should take a five-minute break before continuing. When we get back, we'll go over the rules again."

Everyone started to stand up or gather together to talk. I heard Liz mutter to Jason. "So that was a little intense."

"Don't worry about it—it'll get easier with every

one you do. The trick is relating to them quickly. Like look at what I'm wearing . . ."

I knew all of the kids in the room but spoke to none of them on a regular enough basis to join a cluster now. They were too busy talking about what had just happened anyway—for a minute my pride swelled up, like it used to when I captivated classmates with my stories. But it was doubtful anyone outside of the cafeteria would hear about it, since there hadn't been an actual fight. Even when I won something, I lost, because it was never a big enough deal to be praised for. I stood up and started making my way to the entrance.

"Hey!"

I stopped so Mr. Silva could catch up with me. He pointed a finger in my face.

"I don't want you causing any trouble in the hall, you hear me?"

"I just need to use the bathroom."

There was a pause.

"Sir," I said.

He reached into the breast pocket of his windbreaker and pulled out a pink washroom slip. "You've been warned," he said before giving it to me.

There were two washrooms on this floor: one next to the gym that doubled as the girls' locker room, and one outside Mme. Rizzoli and Mr. Esposito's room.

Ambling over to the one closer to class would let me waste more time, since it was farther from the cafeteria, farther from that unbelievably stupid circle.

I wished I was the kind of person who brought a gel pen to the washroom so I could draw on the stall walls and doors — it would have saved me the trouble of figuring out what to do while I tried to dawdle. Instead I made my way over to the shared sink in the middle of the washroom, stomping on the pedal so that water sprayed out and I could splash my face. When I took my foot off, I heard sniffling. Then sighing. Then swearing.

"There's no toilet paper in this fucking shithole!"

A stall door opened with a whack and Anita stepped out, her eyelashes wet and her nose runny. It took a minute for her to see me but when she did, she jerked to a stop. Her eyes widened then narrowed and she clenched her jaw, clenched her fist, swallowing hard. She was ready. Ready for me to say something. But I could only stare at her. I'd only ever seen her cry once, when she broke her arm in the stairwell trying to jump from a landing to the floor. Getting injured was the only time any of us cried. Or cried in public anyway.

Anita's closed lips trembled like she wanted to say something, but she didn't open her mouth. She was waiting for me to go first. I wanted to laugh at her.

Tease her. Call her soft. I was certain she'd have done that to me if I'd been the one who was caught. It was an urge I could feel with my entire body, like the triumph I'd felt at making her storm out of the cafeteria, the triumph that had made my arms and legs tremble with adrenaline. But I didn't open my mouth to say anything, either.

I don't know how long the two of us stood there before I walked over to the dispenser and ripped off a long piece of paper towel. I held it out for her to take but she stayed where she was. After a few seconds I turned my head to the side so I wouldn't see. Wouldn't see her walk up to me. Wouldn't see her take the paper towel from my hands. Wouldn't see her wipe her eyes and blow her nose and cry a little more into the rough brown tissue. I heard her sigh and knew it was safe to look at her again. Her face was tear-streaked and her eyes were raw and bloodshot; it was like I was seeing her for the first time.

"Wash your face before you leave," I said.

"Oh right. Yeah."

I nodded once and walked back to the door. Maybe before she would've called after me, demanded I keep my mouth shut about what I'd seen. Maybe before I wouldn't have listened if such an order was made. But now neither of us said anything else as I left the washroom to go back to the cafeteria. We both knew that something was different between us and that tomorrow I would be back with the group, but that we'd never speak of this day again.

FIAH KITTY

MY MOTHER LIKES US TO GO TO CHRISTMAS dinner at my grandmother's either very early or very late, just before most of our family shows up or just after a bulk of them leave. It's the one time of year my mother visits Nana's house at all, both of them avoiding each other, speaking only when it's time to exchange gifts. Tonight she decides on early, and we scrape the bottom of our boots against the *Jesus Watches* doormat three times. My mother peers into her cracked black purse, checking to see if she remembered Nana's present—a pair of gloves, black and leather and kind of old-fashioned. When she confirms it's there, she rings the doorbell. I can see her hand tremble slightly. If she catches me noticing she'll build an inward wall that'll take all night to break down, so I rub my hands together and look around the neighbourhood as we wait.

In the summer, giant green maple trees cloak this street in shade but tonight, fallen snow blankets their leafless branches. Nana has draped a string of white lights along the roof of her bungalow and hung a belled wreath just below the peephole on the door. There's even a nativity set on the lawn. It's all picture-perfect, like a drawing on a postcard, but the lurch in my stomach when the front door opens keeps me rooted in reality.

Despite my mother's careful planning, we aren't the only ones here. Two of Nana's friends from Faith Community Baptist Church, Sister Ida and Sister Bernice, have decided to stop by before trudging through the snow to a late-night service. My mother and I will stay for an hour, eat our two plates, and then leave. It's what we always do. Each Christmas, Nana carves a few slices of turkey for us before the grand unveiling of her work at the actual dinner. She's a master at shaving off pieces no one will be able to see when she makes the ceremonious first cut after family prayer. But tonight my mother doesn't seem that interested in eating. She didn't even prep me before we got here, give her annual breakdown on the balance between spending time with Nana and getting out of the house quickly. She only told me to be polite.

"Don't be so eager for the food," she said. "We're guests in her home."

"But we used to live here."

"When you were a toddler." Her tone got mean, like I'd hit a nerve. "What does that have to do with right now, Kara? Hmm? Tell me."

"Nothing," I mumbled.

"Like I said, we are guests in her home so wash your plate when you're done eating, don't just leave it in the sink."

"But she'll just —"

"I know she'll just wash it again, Kara. I know she'll wipe down the table right after you finish eating and she'll spray our boots with Febreze right after we take them off. I *know*. But just do what I say and that's to do what she says."

For now, I sit at the dining table, a bamboo bowl in front of me because Nana has tasked me with making the salad and there's no room left on the counters since the ham is resting there. Sister Bernice is helping her make the sorrel punch in the kitchen to the right of me and even though I haven't sipped it yet, the thought of its tangy, sour taste makes me suck in my cheeks. To my left, my mother sits in the living room and chooses the spot at the far end of the sofa. It's the spot that's closest to the escape, because it's directly across the archway that leads back into the foyer and the front door. Not that I think she'll try to make a break for it or anything but she likes the security of a quick exit.

Nana never turns off the stereo and always keeps the same Christian radio station on low, even if the TV is on, so my mother picks up the remote and turns up the volume.

L'Oréal Kids Shampoo! Oh yeah! Bye-bye tears! No more ouch! No bad hair days! Great shampoo! And shiny hair too! L'Oréal Kids Shampoo, because we're worth it too!

She shifts her hips on the plastic-covered sofa like she's uncomfortable. She does this instead of wriggling her body to get as comfortable as she can, like she normally does when she sits on it.

Sister Ida stands in the opposite corner of the living room, the one by the archway that leads to the bathroom and two bedrooms at the back of the house. The tree fills that corner, the tip nearly touching the ceiling, and Sister Ida slinks around it, admiring the arrangement of ornaments. Nana went all out this year with the baubles and bows, the dangling candy canes and the black angel my mother bought her two years ago because she was sick of looking at the white one Nana always perched on top of the tree. Everything should clash but it works somehow, seducing anyone who looks at it into trying to figure out how it all comes together.

Nana takes the lid off the silver stockpot to check on the rice and peas, and peers into the skillet on the burner next to it. The plantain she's frying makes my stomach grumble and she tells me to grab a saucer so she can give me one or two slices.

"This likkle girl here, she love the plantain, yuh know," she tells Sister Bernice. "It nah Christmas food but mi cook it on Christmas for her. I bring she back to Hanover last year for my niece's wedding, must've been Kara's second visit to Jamaicar. Nothing troubled her when she visit the first time but last year? Lawd. She had a sickness inna her belly that make she chrow up. Only thing she could keep down was plantain and she nah want Bredda's wife plantain, she only want fi eat what mi fry."

She's being chatty. Nana gets that way when she cooks sometimes and when it happens, I wonder if she even knows what she's saying or if words simply tumble out of her as she works, hands moving above all four burners, stirring and mixing, seasoning and adjusting. It would explain why she doesn't know when to *stop* saying things, when she steamrolls over unspoken boundaries and the chattiness turns to shouting.

Sister Ida runs a finger along the garland swirled

around the tree and then smiles as she watches me eat a slice of plantain.

"Eloise, you must have been worried sick," she says to my mother.

She and Sister Bernice have different accents than Nana; they speak in what she calls "the Standard way." It's what makes Rochelle call them stush if we ever run into them at the bus stop outside the McDonald's.

"Oh, Eloise nuh go," says Nana, waving a hand. "She had a, what yuh say, Eloise, yuh had a test? Mi nah remember, but she said it was too important fi miss."

I roll a tiny bit of plantain around my tongue, watching my mother's reaction. There's a tenseness to her face, and I expect her to end this night before fulfilling our tradition—either by telling me it's time to go so as to not make a scene in front of company, or by allowing her anger to eclipse decorum and telling Nana all the ways she is out of line. Instead she looks from Sister Ida to Sister Bernice, smiling tight-lipped and good-mannered.

"That's right," she says. She's working at keeping her tone pleasantly neutral. "I couldn't get an extension for my final exam and if I hadn't taken it, I would've failed the course, which would've interfered with my graduation. I wish I could've gone."

Her hands are clenched fists atop her lap and her

expression stays fixed in one of decided patience. It makes me uneasy. There's a script she's following, but she hasn't thought to tell me what my lines are.

"Ah, no bother." Sister Bernice opens the fridge and puts the pitcher of sorrel on the top shelf. Her church suit, pastel pink and shimmering, distracts me for a minute. It restricts her movements so she bends awkwardly, and to keep myself from smirking, I sit back down at the dining table, taking the saucer of plantain with me.

"The three of you will go again soon. You would like that, right, Kara? Do you like going to Jamaica?"

I don't answer right away. I wish Sister Bernice hadn't addressed me. It's easy being silent, listening to Nana's friends coo over how well-behaved I am and tell my mother how lucky she is to have such an obedient daughter. Let them talk about me and treat me like I'm ten instead of thirteen. Being careful with my words and measuring my tone, speaking at *all*, is harder.

Keeping silent would be much easier if my grandfather were here. George Davis doesn't speak much. To us, his family, he's surly, but to everyone else he's just quiet, and after five minutes of trying to pull words out of him, Nana's friends end up leaving him alone. The very few instances I've been around him and company at the same time, sitting next to him meant I was left alone, too. But it doesn't look like Nana's house is the one he's chosen for Christmas dinner this year.

My mother turns her head slightly toward me so I can see the warning in her eyes. I have to say something soon or I'll go from being seen as well-mannered to being seen as facety, rude, insolent, and then I'll be in trouble for sure.

"Yes, Sister Bernice, I do like going to Jamaica," I say finally. "Last time I was there, Nana taught me how to play cricket in the yard."

Satisfied with my answer, my mother returns her attention to the TV as Nana turns off one of the burners, laughing deep in her belly.

"Mi teach her cricket for true." She eyes the tree from the kitchen and then she sucks up her chortling. "Eh-eh, Ida! Look at how yuh trouble my tree."

Nana leaves the kitchen and walks past me to the living room. When she makes it to the tree, she shifts the garland around the branches.

"Verna, it looks exactly the same as before, come now," says Sister Ida. Her tone is patient and mildly disapproving, but it's no use. Nana has standards that no one but her can meet or anticipate. I've seen it first-hand, lived with it.

When I was four, before my mother moved us to the duplex on Belgravia Avenue, we lived in the basement downstairs. In the early afternoons, long before Nana got back home, I would sneak upstairs into her bedroom and play with the porcelain figurines on her dresser. My father was around at least part-time then, and whenever he caught me putting on my productions — dramatic arguments and theatrical reunions between the milkmaids and young lads — he'd rush me out of the bedroom and tell me to stay in the hall. I'd watch him spend the next ten minutes moving the figurines to the exact same places, at the exact same angles, I'd found them in, and then he'd take me back downstairs and close the door behind us like we'd never surfaced to the top floor at all. Still, when Nana came back home, we could hear her complaining about the way I'd troubled her things. I never understood how she knew after all the work my father had put in.

Sister Ida smooths down the front of her plum church dress and sits down on the opposite side of the couch from my mother, so there's a space in the middle for one more person to sit. I start to chop more quietly so I can hear what they're saying.

"Tell us more about cricket, mm?" she says. "I didn't know you knew enough about cricket to teach your granddaughter."

Nana turns from the tree, pursing her lips the way

she does when she's struggling to hold onto her irritation but can't hold back a smile.

"How yuh say I don't know about cricket? I canna chrow the ball far for true, but I know how fi run," she says, walking back to the kitchen. "I'm fast like. I was the fastest one inna the neighbourhood. No, hear me say, inna the whole parish! That is why they used fi call me 'fiah kitty'!"

That's not what she told me when we were in Hanover last year. Then, she told me that the kids used to call her fiah kitty because of her temper. It was how she tried to warn me against disobeying her. "Yuh saucy, young lady, but I am fiah," she'd said. "You canna boss me, yuh hear—they used fi call me fiah kitty because my temper run hot! Yuh nuh want fi get burned!" She would never be able to hit me, though, and we both knew it. My mother had stripped my grandparents of that right, leaving herself as the only person who could discipline me in that way. But Nana could yell. And the way she quarrelled, the way she seemed to breathe rage, I believed the story.

"It reminds me of Eloise and how she used to run track," says Sister Ida. She reaches across the sofa and taps my mother on the shoulder. "You remember that, Eloise?"

My mother nods and even manages a little chuckle.

It startles me. I can count on one hand the number of times I remember her laughing in this house. "I'm surprised you remember, Miss Ida."

"Oh yes. I remember the old days before we all moved here, how you used to run along Flemington Road, outrunning the boys who thought they could beat you. Fast like the wind this one."

"Must be in the blood then," says Sister Bernice. She's standing right behind my chair now, her hands gripping both finials. "Do you play sports, Kara?" she asks me.

"Hmm?" It comes out lazily, quietly, but my mother hears it from the couch. She refocuses her attention on me, and my cheeks flush with panic.

"I'm sorry, Sister Bernice," I correct myself. "I didn't hear you."

But Nana, beside me again at the stove, answers the question for me.

"Kara nuh like sport," she says. "Eloise, when she was small, she used fi always want to be outside but Kara like fi stay indoors and draw or read, exercise her mind, yuh know? She take after she grandpa."

I know it's a compliment, probably the best kind of compliment to my grandmother. She told me once that my grandfather doesn't have any charm or humour, he has pride and smarts, a mind that likes to learn, and that's why she married him. Still, it feels strange to hear myself be attached to him when he's the person I see the least.

I wonder if Sister Ida and Sister Bernice know that even though my grandparents are married, he only sleeps here when he wants to, that they each lead second lives separate from the other. That Nana's includes church and their friendship, while Grandpa's involves other houses he can attend holiday dinners at. That even though he sees other women, he threw a fit last Christmas when Nana's widower neighbour, Mr. Cardoza, arrived at her house at the same time my mother and I did.

"What man only drops by for a coffee this late at night, Verna?" he'd said.

"Stop fussing. He is just lonely!"

"And why must it be you fi keep him company?"

"Not all men are snakes, yuh know," she'd answered. "Not all men are you."

No, Sister Bernice and Sister Ida probably know nothing about that. That'd be too much of Nana's business for them to be privy to, up there with the bush medicine I'd see her take once in a while and the obeah woman my mother said Nana went to when she was a kid. I'd like to ask them where they think my grandfather is now but instead I watch as my mother reaches into her purse and takes out the gift box she had professionally wrapped at The Bay. She got the kind of quality paper Nana would appreciate, a deep Christmas red, finished with a glittering gold ribbon tied into a bow. There's an envelope I've never seen before taped to the box and my mother unconsciously passes her thumb over it in a back-and-forth motion.

Sister Ida gets up to examine the framed photo of the Royals Nana has hung on the wall, and Sister Bernice goes into the living room to join her. The photo, a black-and-white still of Elizabeth II's wedding to Prince Philip, hangs above the china cabinet in the corner, next to a copy of the Royal Standard of Jamaica. It holds no meaning for me, but my mother sneers at it every time she sees it. But now, Sister Ida and Sister Bernice have somehow started arguing the merits of two cricket players, Frank Worrell and Lawrence Rowe — batsmen, I think. Nana laughs by herself in the kitchen, telling stories about fiah kitty, content with the fact that she is her only listener. I finish putting cucumbers and shredded carrots into the salad and then my mother catches my eye, mouthing my name as a way to call me over to where she's sitting.

I leave my post at the dining table and venture into the living room. She hands me the present with the same trembling hands that rang the doorbell earlier.

"Give this to Nana," she says. "And tell her to read the card now."

By the time I make it back to the kitchen, Nana has taken the turkey out of the oven and heaved the pot onto the stove. She claps her hands together the way she does when she finishes a large task and then acknowledges that she sees me.

"The salad finish?" she asks.

"Oh, yeah," I say.

"Ah wah?" she says, laughing. "Yuh want another chore?"

"No, I mean, sure, maybe later." I don't know where this sense of pressure is coming from, why I feel the weight of my mother's gaze on my shoulders, but it makes me awkward as I speak to her. I hold out the gift in front of me.

"Merry Christmas," I say.

Nana doesn't accept the present right away and I will her to just take it and make things easier on me for once.

"I know we usually put the presents under the tree but it's important that you read the card now," I say.

It's a few more moments before Nana takes the gift box from me. When she does, she gently traces her fingertips over the wrapping paper.

"This is very nice," she says, and I know when she

peels off the wrapping at the end of the night, she'll do so carefully, delicately, so she can use it for something else.

She tears open the cream-coloured envelope to reveal a green Christmas card. On the front, an angel made of swirls and snowflakes holds a trumpet to her lips, blowing out a Bible verse: *And the angel said unto them, Fear not: for behold, I bring you good tidings of great joy, which will be to all people. Luke 2:10.*

Nana nods her head in appreciation before opening the card to read what's written inside. I look back to the living room, and my mother is making a show out of watching TV. Something is about to be different.

Something big.

Nana's expression tells me nothing when she finishes reading and puts the card and present on one of the chairs around the dining table. She moves back to the stove and peers into the stockpot again, using a long wooden spoon to check the rice. After she turns off the burner, she leans to her left and looks at the pendulum clock hanging on the wall above the sink.

"Eh-eh, look at the time!" she says. "Bernice. Ida. Yuh must fi gwine now to catch the evening service. With all this snow and storm and t'ing."

Sister Ida glances at the thin gold watch around her wrist and exclaims at seeing the time.

"Yes, Bernice, we should go," she says.

"Oh all right."

They both wish me and my mother a Merry Christmas and tell us that they'll pray for our prosperity at service. Nana doesn't let them leave before handing them one of the two black cakes she baked. This one doesn't have rum in it, she explains. She walks Sister Ida and Sister Bernice to the door and they spend another five minutes saying their goodbyes before they finally leave. Nana watches them from the oval window for a few seconds and then heads back into the kitchen, opening the cupboard next to the sink.

She pulls out a glass plate, one of her wide and thick ones, then she starts shaving off portions of the turkey, digging out some of the stuffing with a fork afterwards. Three slices on the dish and six forkfuls on the slices. She adds three large spoonfuls of rice and peas, and then two pieces of ham with baked pineapple. The four slices of plantain lets me know this plate is for me. Without a word, she sets it down on a placemat, turns back around to the cupboard, and takes out a small bowl with gold trim, filling it with the salad I spent most of the visit preparing.

I don't try to talk to her while she does this, unveils her art and sets up her masterpiece, while she takes out the bottle of Thousand Island dressing and the pitcher of sorrel from the fridge, setting them on the table by my plate. The anticipation I feel as she takes out an amber drinking glass from the cabinet makes the house feel familiar again, and the unease I've felt since my mother took out Nana's present reverts to a more familiar awkwardness. It's the awkwardness I'm used to and have learned to expect, the awkwardness that fuses with excitement for Christmas dinner.

Nana speaks only after she puts a fork and knife on either side of the glass dish and sets the white gravy boat in the middle of the table.

"Do not forget fi say grace and thank God for his bounty."

She pulls out the chair for me to sit in and when I get settled, she looks across to the living room.

"In the bedroom," says my mother.

Nana leaves the kitchen and my mother gets up from the couch and walks through the archway to the back of the house. A couple of seconds later, I hear the click of a door closing and then nothing but the hymns from the radio and the narration from the TV. *How the Grinch Stole Christmas* is on, the old one, not the one I saw in the theatres a couple of years ago.

. . . Yet in thy dark streets shineth. The everlasting Light. The hopes and fears of all the years. Are met in thee tonight . . .

. . . Fahoo fores, dahoo dores, welcome Christmas, bring

your light. Fahoo fores, dahoo dores, welcome in the cold of night . . .

I sit still for a bit, waiting to hear something from the bedroom. When no shouting rings throughout the house, I close my eyes and clasp my hands together to say grace.

Dear Lord, thank —

I open one eye, straining my ears. Still nothing. I close them again.

Dear Lord . . . Dear Lord . . . Dear Lord, I just want to get through this Christmas with no one dying. Amen.

I pick up my knife and fork but don't do anything with them. The silence from the bedroom is distracting; they've never been this quiet together for this long. An image of them silently struggling for domination, their hands wrapped around each other's throats, flashes in my mind and urges me to push out my chair and get up from my seat.

I haven't wandered this house in years, but I still remember the creak spots on the floorboards from when I was a kid and I tiptoe around them, getting as close as I can to the door while still being far enough to pretend I'm on my way to the washroom if I'm caught.

I hold my breath to better hear what's happening. My mother's voice comes first.

"It's the Christian thing to do."

"*Backside!*" says Nana. "Yuh must really be desperate fi tell me about Christianity."

My mother's words come out wary and measured. "Like I said, there are six months left on the lease but after that . . ." Silence. "I am asking for Kara."

"What about she father? Canna ask him for help?"

A pause.

"When I knew him he could barely help himself, and it's been years since I've known him. Listen, do you really think you aren't my last resort? I am asking for some understanding and some kindness." There's a deep sigh. "It is Christmas, after all."

Silence. For a second I'm scared that I've been found out, that the door will open and they'll find me standing here, but Nana speaks.

"One year, Eloise. Mi ah give yuh one year and one year alone."

I don't hear what she says next. I don't want to hear. As swiftly as I can, I creep back to the kitchen and resume my seat at the dining table. It's only when I pick up my knife and fork again that I realize I'm still holding my breath and I exhale. One year. I pour some gravy onto the turkey. One year living in this house again. I eat a piece of ham. One year living under her rule. I take a bite of plantain. I don't see how we'll survive it, how my mother will survive it.

The door clicks open again and Nana walks into the kitchen first, opening the cupboard and taking out another glass plate. My mother comes in after her and stops behind my chair, bending down to kiss me on the top of my head and stroke the baby hairs curled by my ears. Neither of them says anything.

I take a chance. "What did you two talk about?"

My mother sits down in the chair next to me. "Eat your food," she says.

"Listen to yuh mother," says Nana, putting the rest of the turkey slices onto the plate.

I continue to eat, putting a forkful of stuffing in my mouth. The uneasiness I thought I'd moved past comes back and works through my body, making it difficult for me to swallow. It's hard to know if my mother will even tell me we'll be living here or if one day she'll just turn down Whitmore Avenue, park in the driveway outside, and act as if this is a routine we've been doing for as long as I've been alive. Nana adds the rice and peas to my mother's plate.

"Last year you told me they called you fiah kitty because you had a bad temper," I say. "It didn't have anything to do with cricket."

"Yeah, well she used to tell me it's because her hair turned red in the sun," says my mother. "It changes with every telling."

"So she lies," I say. "She's a liar."

My mother turns to me, a rare quiet anger in her expression. "Apologize," she says. "Apologize to your grandmother right now."

Nana acts like she can't hear us and puts my mother's plate in front of her seat, on the placemat.

"Thank you," says my mother.

She doesn't take her eyes off me and I lower mine then mumble, "I'm sorry, Nana."

Nana makes her way back to the counter. "Mi just like fi tell stories," she says. "Eloise," she looks over to my mother, "maybe Kara get she storytelling from me. Remember when she used fi tell tall tales inna school? When she was small?"

My mother eats some stuffing and nods her head. "I do."

I narrow my eyes at them. They've found something just short of camaraderie with each other, an understanding maybe, an alliance in keeping a secret from me, in *lying* to me. I wonder where it'll all go when one of them finally tells me the truth, how long it'll last when we're all under the same roof again.

My mother nudges me. "Why aren't you eating?"

I shrug and put a large forkful of rice in my mouth as a response.

"Okay, well, since you're not inhaling your food

like you normally do," she says, "change the channel or turn the TV off. This show or movie or whatever it is is annoying."

I get up from the dining table and walk back into the living room, facing the TV. The Grinch starts to smile his famous smile as his dog, Max, frowns, covered in snow.

Then he got an idea. An awful idea. The Grinch got a wonderful, awful *idea!*

I pick up the remote, turn off the TV, and then walk back to the dining table.

"Thanks," says my mother.

I nod as I watch her stuff a piece of turkey in her mouth, as Nana puts the ham back in the oven to warm it up again, those words in my head: An idea. An awful idea. A wonderful, awful idea . . .

INSPECTION

10:30 A.M.

By this time Kara has taken a second shower. The first one was more like a rinse, Eloise says. This time Kara uses the expensive body wash, the one Nana bought her from Crabtree & Evelyn — it smells like rose petals and it exfoliates. Cousins always ask her about it at family outings. It's the only time they ask her about anything.

And don't forget to scrub your underarms. You have a problem with sweating.

I know, Mom. Okay?

Are you using a tone with me?

Sorry.

11:00 A.M.

Applying lotion is important. Kara coats her legs three times. The only thing worse than an unkempt head is ashy elbows and blackened knees. To walk around anywhere with dry skin is to walk around a motherless child, but Kara isn't going just anywhere, she's going back to her old neighbourhood. It's been three weeks since she'd last been to Eglinton West and Marlee, eight months since her mother moved them out of Nana's house to Wilson and Bathurst.

A dry patch on the skin wouldn't attract any stares or whispers, nothing so obvious as to alert Kara to her offence, but soon it would be known that Kara Davis wasn't raised proper. Canna even cream her legs them, the church women would say. And when the murmurs reached Nana, who would leave a voicemail for Eloise, a slap would sting Kara's skin and Eloise would yell, "How do you have no sense that you forgot to cream your skin? Now everyone is talking!"

She makes sure to get in between her fingers and especially the spaces in between her toes. Maybe she'll rub on some baby oil to be safe.

11:10 A.M.

There is an anxious bent to her shoulders now; she never seems to have anything to wear. The outfit she needs is particular. It always has to be, when she goes back to the neighbourhood.

An outfit dressy enough for people to know she has standards, that her mother taught her well and her grandmother before her, but plain enough so they won't sneer behind her back. It's a balance her neighbourhood friends say she's never mastered.

It's July, and hot. Wear a sundress, says Eloise. Like the ones those bohemian girls wear. The Erykah Badu one.

Kara only has one dress like that: the turquoise one that people say is coloured like the ocean. She prefers jeans, even shorts, but she doesn't feel like arguing and puts the dress on anyway. She hates it.

She hates the way it falls on her like it's a sheet. Hates the way it accentuates her lack of breasts, lack of curves, lack of the voluptuous beauty that makes her aunts and cousins laugh behind their hands and say, Yuh sure yuh a Jamaican gyal?

She doesn't stand in the mirror too long.

11:45 A.M.

The anxiety in Kara's shoulders morphs into pure fear. The real battle has approached.

Her hair.

It's been a week since she has combed it out; she

hasn't been anywhere important, just the Pizza Pizza by Collinson Boulevard and the twenty-four-hour coin laundry by Laurentia Crescent while her mother went to the Money Mart across the street. She clenches and gasps and grunts and groans as she wields the comb, ripping through a thicket of knots and tearing through clumps of tangles, trying to uncoil the ringlets before they scrunch back up into tight curls. Her scalp is raw; she may be getting a headache. Spraying on texture softener isn't fast enough. She takes the nozzle off of the bottle of *Just for Me* and dumps it all over her head, rubbing it into her roots.

Her hair starts to take shape. It's only acceptable. She can already see the raised eyebrows from the women also going natural, their beautifully sculpted 'fros, black bouquets of hydrangeas atop their heads. Every time she sees them, she wants to yell at them to stop side-eyeing her knotted curls.

12:30 P.M.

Sweat starts to prickle Kara's underarms and she reapplies the deodorant Eloise gave her, the one actually made for men, and then sprays on some perfume for good measure. She adjusts her dress so her bra doesn't show. Last time she visited the neighbourhood, boys spotted a patch of pink lace and followed her for a block and a half. The attention was a twisted phenomenon. Boys ignored the skinny girls: no breasts, no real ass, nothing to bark at. But still they followed her, laughing and catcalling: Damn girl, can I getta piece o' dat? With each step she'd taken she prayed that they'd leave her alone, but was pleased to have a discomfort to report to her friends. According to them, this was what it was to be a woman.

The old-timer women had looked at her with pursed lips, raising their eyebrows like she was having sex right there on the street for children and God to see. She was too afraid, too guilty, to try to see if any of them knew anyone from her family and decided it was best to go home before something happened that she couldn't take back.

12:32 P.M.

It's time for inspection.

Eloise tells Kara to stand back so she can see her better, so she can see the full effect of what Kara put together.

You put deodorant on?

Nod.

You brush your teeth?

Nod.

You put lip gloss on?

Nod.

Hmm.

Eloise isn't convinced. She never is. But Kara thinks she looks fine. Her look, almost prepubescent, is perfect, she thinks. No cars will slow down for her, no church ladies will whisper "slack" when they see her dress, because it reaches her ankles and doesn't stop mid-thigh.

Eloise gets up from the couch and takes a few steps toward Kara so that she's standing a few inches from her face.

If you see someone we know, make sure to call her ma'am.

I will.

And if you see someone from our family, don't talk our business.

I won't.

If your fast friends start talking to some boys, leave and meet them somewhere when they're done.

Of course.

And bring me back something to eat. Jerk chicken and rice.

Yes, Mom.

Kara heads for the door and feels Eloise's eyes watching her, searching her body for an imperfection to catch and correct. Kara knows that Eloise is running through a list in her head, making sure she hasn't missed any instruction or overlooked any direction, making sure she won't get a phone call later in the afternoon about her daughter's raggedy appearance or unruly behaviour. Kara turns around and tells her she knows the protocol, that she's been listening for the past two hours, for the past fourteen years. She tells Eloise that it's all in her head.

12:40 P.M.
Ready.

BRANDON & SHEILA

OUR NEIGHBOUR WAS A DRUG DEALER. OR AT least *I* thought he was a dealer; my mother just thought he was Brandon, a spoiled twenty-year-old white boy with spoiled twenty-year-old white boy problems. She said it was the way he fidgeted beneath his baggy clothes, the way he twisted his mouth to put on an accent — those things exposed him. He'd run away to Wilson and Bathurst, she said, hiding out in the apartment across from ours as a way to rebel against Mommy and Daddy.

"Both things can be true," I'd say.

My mother would shake her head. "Doesn't look like he has the stomach for it."

"Oh sure he does — listen." My hands would start

moving to help me make my point. "He needs to make a living somehow and he doesn't have the stamina for manual labour."

"Or maybe he *is* getting money from his parents," I'd revise, "but just enough to pay for rent and groceries. They probably think he's in the city for school or something."

We'd make up stories like these whenever we heard a disturbance coming from his side of the hall, which was all of the time. The walls in this building were thinner than the ones in our old duplex on Belgravia Avenue and definitely thinner than the ones in Nana's house. Even if we hadn't been fascinated with Brandon's life, we wouldn't have been able to escape its drama.

Whenever I got to our apartment and could hear that my mother had arrived home before me, I'd stand outside our door and brace myself for the cross over the threshold, steadying my breath as I went over a list in my mind, a list of potential wrongdoings that would trigger an argument. Sometimes I counted to ten in my head, and then sometimes, mid-count, two or three gaunt-faced men would arrive and bang on Brandon's door until he opened it and then they'd push their way inside. Immediately after, nineties dancehall would start blasting so it was nearly all we could hear next door. It was the only time Brandon bothered with music to mask his interactions. But even then, when there was yelling we could still hear snippets of the arguments, and it was Brandon's voice we heard the most.

"Nah, fuck that, man. He's lying, bro. I fucking swear he's lying. Y'all are my bredren, right? My homies? I wouldn't fucking do that, I swear everything is criss as shit!"

"This is why he's a dealer," I'd say to my mother. "Maybe one who is over his head, but still, a dealer."

My mother only conceded that he was probably a user. He was definitely a partier. The night he moved in he knocked on our door and politely told us that he'd be having a few people over to his place. My mother thanked him for letting us know. After that, dusk-till-dawn ragers were regular occurrences, and our living room stank of the weed they'd smoke. I asked her once why she didn't threaten to set the landlord on them like she'd done in the other apartments we'd lived in. She looked at me, her eyes somehow weary and sharp at the same time, and sighed.

"Because I'm tired, Kara."

Tonight, Brandon was arguing with Sheila. She hadn't been around for a while. The love Brandon had for Sheila was kind of scary, and the love she had for him was kind of psychotic. He kicked guests out of his apartment for touching her knee, threw what had to be lamps or vases or glass ashtrays across the room. Sob. Howl. Then they'd fuck. He'd kick her out after. She'd smash a window and break back in, threaten to "fuck up" any new girlfriend he might find, scream that she loved him when he said he couldn't believe she slapped girls just for saying "hi." The first time I saw her, the same night Brandon moved in, she looked quiet, subdued. Short. Blonde. A pink streak in her hair. White, like translucent white, like she'd never been in daylight. I couldn't picture her hysterical with rage. But we heard it every night. Maybe Brandon just did that to her.

Keeping track of Brandon's relationship with Sheila became a sort of game my mother and I were all too eager to play. We'd turn down our TV to hear their fights better and come up with all kinds of drama for them to scream at each other about. But tonight, it was different. I didn't want to guess their crisis; I wanted to listen.

"You fucking asshole, Brandon! You're a goddamn fucking asshole!"

"Sheila, shut up! There's a fourteen-year-old girl next door!"

Up until now my mother had been sitting quietly in the armchair. I'd chosen to do my homework at the breakfast table across the room in the kitchen, which was really a couple of cupboards, an oven, and a tiny counter. The small space between us was full of what we could cram into this studio: a sofa bed and coffee table, our cherry-wood TV cabinet. Even from across the apartment, I could tell that her eyes were fixed on me.

"How does he know you're fourteen?"

"Mom, I'm not fourteen. I'm sixteen."

She hadn't forgotten. She just wanted to catch me in a lie. It was what she'd do when I was younger — say something, anything, and see how I'd respond to it. As a kid I'd made the mistake of offering up overly complicated explanations, thinking that the more detailed I was, the more her doubt would ebb. Those explanations usually ended up revealing some kind of secret I wasn't even aware I was keeping from her. Now I knew to say as little as possible.

She'd been suspicious of me since I'd come home, watching me, scanning my movements. I knew she was filing away my every gesture to pick apart and replay before going to bed. Most of our fights happened moments after we turned off the lights. That was when everything was clear, when she knew what she really wanted to argue about, and she couldn't fall asleep with unanswered questions crowding her mind. Or at least that was what she told me. But we hadn't had a fight in almost two weeks, which was the longest we'd ever gone without her yelling at me. I didn't want the fact that she was fishing for a confession about a boy — Terrence — to ruin our delicate peace.

But I couldn't tell her about the kiss.

EARLIER THAT DAY, after school, Terrence Peters had shoved his tongue down my throat. First he'd asked if he should do it — just to see if everyone was right about us and we really were secretly in love with each other, he said. Terrence was the only other black kid in my grade ten English class, and we were always put together when Ms. Garrison broke us into pairs for exercises. The other students migrated to one another, leaving us as the only possible partners for the other, and since it kept happening, we'd just decided to become friends. We didn't realize the entire school would assume we were dating.

When the bell had ended the last period, he'd found me by the library and took me by the wrist. Wordlessly, he led me up the stairwell no one really used, the one that led to the fifth floor of the school, dedicated to a now-abandoned art room.

"Hi," he said.

"Hi."

He was quiet for a bit and then he started talking, avoiding my gaze and shrugging his shoulders a lot.

"Haven't you ever thought about it?" he asked. "Maybe we should just kiss."

Terrence didn't date much, but when he did he picked girls who made me question if I was at least average. All flowy blonde hair, big-breasted and perky. Nothing I aspired to, but a brand of pretty that turned guys into idiots, which was something I couldn't help but notice. I'd grumble at seeing Terrence's dumb, slackened face after he'd kissed one of those girls. He'd lost his virginity to one of them, and when he'd told me about it in morning period, I hadn't spoken to him for the rest of the day.

I looked at him, slanted there against the railing. He was tall and curly-haired. He had skin smooth and dark like molasses. Cute. Even my mother had said so when I'd introduced him to her at parent-teacher night a few months ago; but her tone was accusatory. She'd sent me here for high school because of the high university-acceptance rates, but the kids who went here worried her. Their parents thought they were entitled to a freedom that led to sex and mouthing off and sex and bad manners and more sex, she said, and she reminded me whenever she could that I had no such liberties under her roof. The way her eyebrow cocked at Terrence that night had let me know that those reminders were going to become even more frequent.

I told him he could kiss me, and then he inched forward and meshed his lips with mine; they would've been soft if he'd remembered to rub on some Vaseline after gym, but they were chapped and dry, rough to feel. My own lips were still puckered when he started to open his mouth. He pressed the tip of his tongue against my teeth until I unclenched them and allowed him access. I couldn't figure him out. He opened his mouth when I closed mine; I thought he'd tilt his head one way, but then we'd bend our necks at the same angle and our lips would rub uselessly together. The sound of our smacking invaded my ears but he didn't seem to mind it; maybe I was wrong to be so aware. He slipped his hands around my waist, and I tried to reciprocate his enthusiasm somehow, remembering the rich moaning I'd sometimes hear coming from Brandon's apartment, but I couldn't bring myself to make that noise. I hunched my shoulders instead, trying to show eagerness, and twirled my tongue around his, but he got excited and shoved his tongue so far down my throat I gagged. I pulled away.

"You okay?" he asked.

"Mm-hmm."

"Good, huh?"

I wondered if I had teeth marks above and below my lips. "Yeah," I said.

He smiled at me roguishly and I indulged him with what I hoped looked like a satisfied grin.

The day Chris kissed my friend Rochelle, they were behind the 7-Eleven at Eglinton and Locksley. He'd grabbed her Mountain Dew Slurpee and taken a sip from her straw, she told me. She teased him about germs, saying it was like they were kissing, and he'd leaned in, slipping his tongue over hers and whispering in her ear, "Nah. That's like kissing."

Anthony and Anita's first kiss had been on a train heading to Yorkdale Mall. She'd been standing next to his seat when the train stopped short, making her fall into Anthony's lap. After a moment's hesitation he pushed his lips against hers.

"It was cool," she'd told us with a shrug and a crack of her bubble gum.

Both times had been two years ago. Anita and Rochelle had made a show of casual retelling, but as they spoke their eyes had watched mine for a flicker of amazement. I knew from how they'd tried not to grin that the way the kisses had happened was just as important as the actual kissing. So I planned to tell them that Terrence had pressed me up against a locker and then made his move. That it was spontaneous and smooth all at once. Really we were on a stairwell landing, no lockers in sight, but Anita and Rochelle wouldn't know that. My mother had chosen to send me to high school on Mount Pleasant, and they were friends from my old neighbourhood—they'd never come down here to scope out my school. And they were both so much further along than me now—Anita was having sex, and Rochelle had let her newest boyfriend touch her over the panties. My first kiss had to have a certain level of sexy.

"A teacher could come up here or something," I said. "I have to get home anyway."

Terrence took my hand as we headed out of the school and I wondered if this meant I'd signed some kind of non-verbal contract, indebting me to something. I didn't ask. Really, I wanted to grab him by the front of his jacket and thrust my face into his, try to make myself moan like Sheila; but maybe that would intensify the terms of our possible contract. Maybe it implied sex: giving myself over to him in a way that made my heart thud.

Outside, he squeezed my knuckles with his fingers and I loosened my own grip on his hand, suddenly aware that we were out in the open where anyone could see us. No one really knew my family around here, but I could never snuff out the fear that my mother would be around the next corner, that a church friend of Nana's would randomly pass by. It had been months since my mother and I had spoken to my grandmother, but a friend telling her she saw me with a boy would be enough for her to call my mother's cell, for her to get over the pride of her silence.

I pretended I needed to stretch and put my hands in my coat pockets.

"Cold," I said.

"Okay." Terrence nodded.

I glanced at his hand. Now that I had let go of it, I wanted nothing more than to take it again. Whenever my mother caught me checking out a storefront boy, she'd put her hands on my shoulders and push me to move faster, set her jaw like she wanted to hit me or shake me, her eyes panicked, almost afraid, afraid that I wanted something that could ruin me, break me like it had tried to break her. Terrence wasn't a storefront boy, but I was doing with him the things I sometimes imagined doing with one of them. A sourness burned in my gut and I opened my mouth to breathe better, trying not to betray the guilt and the curiosity I was feeling toward Terrence. I knew my mother could straighten me out if I told her about the kiss, untangle me, clarify things somehow, but not before the yelling, yelling that could split the cordial silence between us, and I didn't want to give up the quiet.

. . .

BUT THE MOMENT I'd walked into the apartment that evening, my mother could tell that something was wrong.

She was sitting in the armchair, using one hand to underline sections of her doctoral research with red pen and the other to rub the left temple of her forehead.

"You look different," she said.

"No, I'm fine." I unlaced my boots and walked over to the breakfast table, moving the takeout bags to the other side so I could put my textbooks down. "How was your day?"

"You look like you're going to be sick."

"I'm fine."

"You fail a math test or something?"

"I said I'm fine."

"Are you using a tone with me?"

"No, Mummy."

She looked at me a bit, tapping the pen against her chin. "Because if there was anything wrong with you, you'd tell me."

"Yeah. Of course," I said.

"Yeah. Of course," she repeated.

The rest of the evening was spent in silence—until Brandon got home, Sheila in tow. Soon he was throwing things because Sheila had slept with somebody named Trevor, either his brother or his friend, I couldn't tell. She wouldn't answer his questions of, "Did you? Well did you? You bitch, you did didn't you?" but only kept yelling, "I saw you with that skank Tessa-fucking-Miller, Brandon." They cared so much about each other I was sure they'd kill one another before separating for good. I didn't know if I wanted something that powerful, if I could even have it with someone, what it would require. Terrence and I had said nothing to each other as he'd walked me to the bus stop from school. I didn't know if he'd resolved what he needed to when he kissed me, or if he'd need me to figure things out again. I didn't know if I wanted to be needed. It didn't seem too far off from being used.

Sheila bellowed. "STOP IT!"

It sounded like Brandon was ramming his fist into a wall. I'd stopped trying to concentrate on biology a while ago and was now only holding my pen for show.

"Do you think she did it?" said my mother. The sharpness of her tone startled me and I flinched.

"What?" I asked.

She looked up from her papers to stare at me, the corners of her mouth tightened.

"I'm sorry," I said. "Pardon?"

"Do you think Sheila cheated with Trevon?"

"I thought it was Trevor."

"The name isn't the point. Do you think she cheated?"

I didn't know. I didn't think it mattered. If it wasn't Trevor or Trevon it'd just be something or someone else. "Sure," I said. "Maybe. I don't know."

My mother scoffed. "You're quiet tonight."

"No, I'm fine," I said, trying to keep my voice even, my breathing settled.

"I always find out, Kara," she said. "Just something to consider."

WE DECIDED TO try again the next day during lunch period. The burnouts usually claimed the stairwell for that hour but for some reason we had it to ourselves. Terrence was good with them, like how he was good with every clique, the one black guy the entire school seemed to love. I had to wonder if he'd arranged it so they wouldn't be here, if he'd told them he needed the privacy to get lucky.

"I wouldn't do that," he said.

But that wouldn't be something he would just admit to.

"Kara, I *wouldn't* do that."

He kissed me. This time he moved down to my neck. All I felt were big wet splotches on my skin, and the sound his mouth made reminded me of a plunger. I didn't know what to do with my hands; Rochelle and

Anita never spoke about that. Once, Brandon had left his apartment to take out the trash, wearing nothing but loose workout shorts. I saw scratch marks behind his shoulder blades. But this didn't feel like the appropriate moment for that kind of response. Abruptly, Terrence's lips found a spot that made me want to sigh and a panicked guilt flared in my chest. I bit down on my teeth to stop myself from gasping. When I felt the urge to grip his shirt I pushed him away.

It hadn't been until the end of the day, when I walked into the first-floor bathroom, that I saw my reflection in the mirror. A dark red splotch marred my neck.

I ran into the library — luckily, no twelfth-graders were hogging the computers at the back of the room. I logged onto MSN and wrote frantically to Rochelle. She had a cellphone now, so she'd get the message right away.

SHIT!!!! 😐😐

. . .

. . .

Wassup??

I typed out what'd happened, and she told me to stop freaking out, that she and Anita would meet me at the Shoppers Drug Mart by Eglinton and Briar Hill, halfway between our schools. It meant taking a different route, a longer route home.

Just tell ur mom tht traffic waz bad!

I spent the bus ride pulling my braids to the side as a way to cover my neck, ignoring how they chafed against my skin. When I met Rochelle and Anita in the Shoppers Beauty Boutique, I touched the braids to make sure they were still in place.

"Stop messing with it," said Rochelle, moving my hand away.

Anita leaned against the Dior shelf, her black JanSport knapsack by her feet. A sales associate hovered at the end of the aisle, carefully casual as she glanced over toward us.

"This is the third time someone has come by here," said Rochelle.

Anita gestured to her bag. "Nothing but textbooks," she said loudly.

I made an exaggerated sigh and said, equally loudly, "I was *thinking* about getting a lipstick but there's something about the service here, it makes me uncomfortable to shop."

The sales associate left, and Anita rolled her eyes toward me. "Anyway," she said. "Back on topic: it's Makeout Session 101, Kara. No teeth."

"Anita, leave it," said Rochelle. "You're supposed to be helping."

"No but really, what did she think was going to

happen?" She turned to me, her eyebrows furrowed in harsh amusement. "You feel the bite, you tell him to back off. Likkle gyal t'ink she bad. Hmph."

"Well, sorry, Anita," I said. "Not all of us are as experienced as you."

"But *wait*." Anita started to move toward me, but Rochelle put herself in between us and told her to relax.

Anita raised her hands in surrender, and I stared at the wall of foundation, irritated but not scared. Not of Anita anyway — we all knew she wouldn't actually lay hands on me. But the lack of brown shades on the shelves made me clench my hands into anxious fists, my nails cutting into my palms. What I did see had prices that would blow half my allowance for the week, and I didn't even know if the shades would match. I couldn't describe my own skin tone; people called me yellow. People who were nicer called me caramel. I had no idea what that translated to in powders.

"Here, get this one," said Anita, groaning slightly. She picked up a bronzing powder. When I stared at her, she sighed. "It's pretty much your exact skin tone."

"No, it has to match perfectly," I said. "It has to fool my mother. And nothing fools Eloise."

"It's the closest you're going to get," said Rochelle. "It'll be fine. You should have this anyway. I don't know how you can show up to school with no makeup on."

I took the compact from Anita and dragged my feet down the aisle to the checkout counter.

"Why aren't you doing this with Terrence?" said Anita. "He's the one who mauled you, he should have to pay for the cover-up."

"I didn't tell him about it."

"You should've," she said. "Guys get proud about their bruising."

I looked at Rochelle and she shrugged. "Anita's right. Don't question it."

IT WAS NEARLY eleven thirty now, and screams of "Brandon! Yes! Brandon!" attacked the walls. I lay awake listening to them while my mother snored next to me on the bed. What excited me about Sheila's screams also terrified me, that kind of abandon that only seemed to exist when they were having sex, the way they almost begged each other for it because for both of them it was a time, a moment that was the best they could ever get and once it was over, everything would fall to shit. But all sex couldn't be like that. The way Anita described it, nothing about it seemed that serious. To my mother, everything about it was ser-ious — at least everything that came after. She never spoke about sex itself; just about how when it was over, people saw each other differently. Men left and women turned steel-eyed.

"Like me. Want to end up like me?" she'd say.

I looked at her next to me. Even asleep, her face was stern and active. She hadn't questioned me when I'd gotten home this time, she just didn't take her eyes off me, surveyed me so I could stew in the guilt she knew I felt but couldn't yet prove. I thought about waking her up and confessing about the kiss. Both kisses. I thought about asking her to yell at me later but advise me now, to tell me about boys, to tell me about what life was like for her when she was my age, a year before she became steel-eyed and hard-hearted. I wanted to know about desire: if having it and receiving it meant that your sense of self was gone; if there was anything romantic in melding with another person, like Sheila and Brandon. I knew she had the answers. I knew she'd be able to reach in and sort me out even if I hated her for it.

There was a jerk, and my mother kicked her foot out. Maybe she was falling in her dream. She opened her mouth and her heavy breathing turned harsh and deep. It was just a noise.

I rolled onto my side so the snoring wouldn't be so loud.

STANDOFF

THE DAY AFTER NANA FOUND OUT MY GRAND-
father still saw his girlfriend there was no extra
food in her house. Any leftover broccoli pie or curry
chicken and rice and peas had been packed away in plastic containers and marched down to Faith Community
Baptist Church: she'd given it all to Pastor to serve at
his soup kitchen on Friday afternoon. After her first
trip — she couldn't carry it all in one — Nana called my
mother to unburden her frustrations. That was how I
knew things were different this time. Nana had ignored
months' worth of their agreed-upon silence in order to
make that phone call.

My mother flipped through *HOMES* magazine the
entire time they were talking. I'd rifled through it

myself once, when I was bored and our cable was disconnected again. In the middle sections I'd discovered calculations and budgets she'd scrawled in the margins and instantly felt like I'd violated a secret, intruded on a private dream. Now I pretended not to notice those blue scribbles as my mother turned the page, peeling it behind the magazine's spine, absently nodding her head to Nana's complaints. I was sitting on the sofa bed across the room but could still hear every word of Nana's garbled ranting through the receiver. She was yelling about the money my grandfather had been lending "that skettle gyal," about the church ladies seeing the two of them walk down the street together, his arm snaked around her waist.

"That man have some nerve, Eloise! Hear me say, him have some *nerve*! Yuh know him always say how him have no money, how him canna give me one, two, t'ree hundred dollar for the mortgage or for the grocery them. But him have money for that *woman?* Eh-eh, him must thank God me a Christian woman, that is all me ah say!"

"Mm-hmm."

"Sister Ida and Sister Rose look 'pon him and that woman too, yuh know! I canna even show my face around the church! Oh my God, that man is selfish, him nuh think about anyone but himself. What they must be saying about me!"

My mother didn't tell her to kick his sorry ass out like I've heard her counsel her friends more than once, but instead fixed her eyes on a particular page in the magazine. When Nana ended the call half an hour later, my mother joined me on the mattress, handing me a takeout menu.

"I think I feel for Chinese," she said.

I didn't open the Ho-Lee-Chow pamphlet. "You could've told her to leave him."

"I have told her to leave him. I've told her since I was your age, maybe a year older."

I could see the scene in my mind too: Nana at the kitchen counter, furiously chopping some thyme or some pepper, pretending not to hear my mother's conviction, pretending not to see the swollen belly on her seventeen-year-old daughter.

"It's depressing that she won't leave him," I said. "Don't you think it's depressing?"

"Maybe I would," said my mother. "If it wasn't so familiar."

SATURDAY AFTERNOON I was at the mall. Yorkdale, not the Eaton Centre; one was ten minutes away from home, the other was forty-five, and I had to stay close to the apartment in case my mother wanted me home before four o'clock. I spent my time soliciting stores, handing managers resumés that took up half a page.

I wasn't supposed to be doing this. According to my mother, school was my only job. It was why she'd sent me to high school and grade school downtown, with junior high in our neighbourhood as a kind of truce in between. But most of my friends had jobs now. Aishani worked at the McDonald's at Lawrence Square, and after she'd spent two cheques on a cellphone, Rochelle and Anita started doing concession at the SilverCity. Only Jordan and I were unemployed. My mother had already bought me a phone, a way to keep tabs, so I didn't know what I would buy if I ever got a job. I didn't know how I would even work a job I wasn't supposed to have. I just liked the idea of money. My money. Of having something I could control.

I only stayed at the mall for an hour. It'd been two weeks since I'd seen Aishani or anyone else, and we said we'd meet up today around one. That was the plan.

I headed toward the subway at noon, but the train stalled on the outdoor track between Lawrence West and Glencairn stations. I was in a window seat and through the glass I looked at the fences atop small, yellowing hills—barrier walls between the houses and the trains. They'd been there forever. It was all cleaned up now but there used to be graffiti on the panels—mostly *fuck you*s or crew symbols, but occasionally I'd see an asymmetrical heart or a love tag: *Tess & Ryan. Josh + Jessica.* As a kid I'd make up stories about those couples. In my mind they were always grunge: all ripped jeans and flannel shirts and loose cargo pants. Sometimes Tess and Ryan snuck out of their bedrooms and hopped the fence; they'd whisper to each other about their love, about their plans, and then they'd spray-paint their names in commemoration. Other times Josh fucked up—maybe he was caught with another girl, maybe he'd said some things in a fight, and he would tag the fence to get Jessica's attention.

I nearly missed my stop and quickly walked onto the platform before the doors slid shut, staring at the *Eglinton West* pasted onto the brown-tiled wall in white letters. I'd planned to make my way to Fairbank Park, maybe twirl idly on the tire swing until everyone came—but I found myself outside of Nana's bungalow instead. She answered the door in a floral housedress with a magenta bra strap sliding off her shoulder.

"This how yuh wear yuh hair now, eh?" she said, eyeing the tight curls spiralling out of my printed head wrap. "I suppose that's the fashion. Natural like, nuh true?"

Her own hair was clipped up and swirled around pink spongy rollers. She had on no lipstick or foundation. I'd only ever seen her like this first thing in the morning, before the sun had made its introduction and the house was still cloaked in sleepy darkness. After nine o'clock, Nana always had to look presentable.

She led me into the foyer. The sound was what I noticed first. Everything was turned off. No scripture from the radio. No whirring of the air conditioner. There was only the stiff ticking of the anniversary clock in the living room. I could hear the creak of my footsteps on the wood of the floor. The smell I noticed second: briny-infused air. Freshly fried saltfish. Nana had cooked recently. She kept walking straight, through the small foyer to the kitchen, as I slipped out of my running shoes, putting my hand against the wall to steady myself. My palm pressed against the full-length mirror Nana had hung by the door, the one I'd kept forgetting was there even when we'd lived with her. She didn't remind me to line up my sneakers on the shoe mat. She didn't scold me for smudging the mirror with my fingertips. My body hummed with unease.

I turned left, into the living room, and then stopped on the spot. My grandfather was sitting, slouched, on the plastic-covered sofa directly across from me. I hadn't expected him to be here after Nana had called my mother to cuss him stink. But here he was, his hands atop his long legs, facing forward. It wasn't a casual position; it was more like a pose. When I took another step into the room, I saw that he was watching a movie on mute. *Dirty Harry.* I stood there for a while, gawking at the scene in front of me before saying something.

"Hi, Grandpa."

His eyes moved from the screen to my face in acknowledgement and then they stared at the television again.

Tick. Tick. Tick.

The clock was next to the stereo in the media cabinet. It was gold and encased in a glass dome. I shifted my weight. Nana puttered around in the kitchen, quieter than normal — but the noise was enough to make me flinch.

"I haven't heard from you guys in a while, so . . ."

This time my grandfather didn't look away from the TV.

"Kara." Nana waved me over.

The dining table separated the kitchen and the living room. I pushed a chair even farther beneath the table, then squeezed past the rounded edge and joined her in front of the sink. All of the counters were empty. There were no silver bowls of bananas or mangoes or plums. Nana usually arranged cereal boxes on top of the fridge but there was no Raisin Bran or Special K; even the Frosted Flakes she always bought on the off-chance I made an overnight visit was nowhere to be seen. There were a few freshly washed dishes in the dish rack: one frying pan, one plate, one fork, and one knife.

"I just stopped by to see how you were."

Nana harrumphed and then lowered her voice. "He nuh move from that seat all day, yuh know. *All day*. He nah even watch that TV."

"I don't get it," I said. "Nana, you own the house. Can't you just tell him to leave?"

"Eh-eh and speak to him?" She shook her head. "Kara, listen when I tell you say, I would rather die than talk to that man."

I opened my mouth but couldn't find anything to say. Each stroke of the living room clock set my teeth on edge and I glared at it. Nana followed my gaze but her eyes landed on my grandfather. He still sat looking straight ahead, as if he was the only one in the house. Nana turned toward the dish rack but not before crinkling her nose into a sneer, her lips furled. I realized then that it wasn't sorrow that kept her from dressing like she normally did: it was spite.

"Nana, if you just—"

"What you want fi eat?" She opened a drawer and put the cutlery away. "Nuh have any food in the house but I can pick up a patty for yuh at the store."

"That isn't why I came."

"Wait here and me gwine fi get."

"Fine."

She put the frying pan away and then took a step closer to me, leaning in to whisper into my ear. "He's stealing my things, yuh know."

I blinked. "What?"

"I know him hide my blow-dryer and my purple Sunday shoes. Him move all my furniture around. Him ah try fi drive me crazy," she hissed.

"Wait, are you serious?"

But she was already walking out of the kitchen, heading to her bedroom at the back of the house to get changed. The living room looked fine. Everything seemed in place. Nothing was missing: not the British teacups in the cabinet or the painted figurines arranged on the coffee table or the Royal Standard of Jamaica pinned above the china cabinet. But I sat down next to my grandfather anyway, the plastic crinkling beneath my weight. I didn't say anything for a while because that had always been our routine whenever we did see each other. We'd sit together in silence, and if we were in front of the television, he would hand me the remote without saying anything, offering me the chance to change the channel from one of his Westerns to one of my sitcoms. I'd usually let him finish the movie before turning to something else. Even now, the longer I sat next to him, the looser my body felt, which was always how it was with me and him. Comfortable. I cleared my throat and took the remote out of his hand and turned the television off.

"So, Nana thinks that you're stealing from her." I didn't feel the need to be careful with my words. Not with him. "Not money or anything, just, you know, everyday stuff."

He shrugged. It was a slow and heavy motion. My grandfather was a tall and thin man but he wasn't nimble. Nana was the opposite of all he was. She was short and loud, stout in both personality and frame, but she was quick-footed, always appearing to be in more than one place at once. My grandfather never seemed to move.

"Just tell me," I said. "You wouldn't do that, right? You wouldn't steal her blow-dryer or move the furniture . . ."

I knew before I'd finished the sentence. I'd known before I even started speaking—but I'd wanted him to kiss his teeth and wave me away, to tell me he was too busy to do something so carefully cruel. Instead he turned his head to look at me and then raised his eyebrows.

I climbed onto the floor, bending into a crouch. The sofa had been pushed back a few inches. I could see the sink marks from where the legs used to be. I shuffled over to look at one of the armchairs; it'd been moved a few inches to the right. The cabinet had been shifted forward.

He'd barely moved anything. He'd adjusted the furniture just enough for the living room to be exactly the same and completely different, just enough for it to look unchanged to anyone but Nana, who knew the precise location of all of her belongings. I stood up, my hands trembling.

"Don't you have anything better to do with your time? Don't you think you're too old for this?"

"Nope."

"You're pushing sixty."

"So?"

"Jesus Chr—"

He glared at me from the corner of his eye, and I pressed my lips together. "Give it all back," I said. "Everything you took from her."

He didn't respond, and I took a step closer to him.

"Are you listening to me?"

"You tell her fi start cook?"

"You have got to be kidding."

He picked up the remote and turned *Dirty Harry* back on.

"You're crazy," I said. "Both of you are crazy."

"You are the one that's crazy," he said.

I shook my head. "George, you're in the wrong here."

"Things are the way things are." I could hear his accent more clearly. He was getting angry. "Yuh nah know everything, yuh know."

A door opened at the back of the house. Nana sauntered through the kitchen without looking at the living room. Her hair was out of the rollers and twirled into nice curls, her body snug in a patterned white-and-turquoise dress. When she made it to the foyer, she called me over again.

"Nana, what now?"

She nodded her head to the entryway closet. There had to be at least twenty jackets in there. Frocks and pea coats in shades of black and green, reefers in navy blue. On the floor, there were rows of pumps and boots lined on a two-level shoe rack, and above the hangers there was a shelf of shawls and headscarves.

"My turquoise shawl is gone. Him take all my nice things because he knows I need fi go out and he nuh want me fi look good. But everyone must see that I look good, everyone must see that I am fine!"

"They're your things. Just demand them back."

She ignored me. "Yuh still like that sweet drink, that Kola Champagne?"

I sighed. "Sure. Yes."

"I'll be back."

Nana left the house, shutting the front door firmly behind her. The sound was swallowed whole by the silence. I didn't leave the foyer and only turned to face the living room. The clock ticked one fifteen. It had only been half an hour since I got to this house. A scream swelled and waned in my chest.

"I guess you just always do what you want," I said.

"Likkle pickney," said my grandfather, turning the volume up on the television. "Why yuh think yuh know everything?"

"I don't." My voice was barely louder than a gasp. "Trust me, I don't."

NIGHTS WHEN MY mother felt restless, either from boredom or frustration, we went out driving like we always did. Sometimes she took Yonge to Front Street and we followed Lake Ontario to the city's outskirts. Other nights, we went past the suburbs to the boonies, cranking the stereo up to full blast as we sped down empty dirt roads. That night, we went to Sheppard and Yonge, and zigzagged in and out of crescents and avenues and cul-de-sacs. Uptown was my least favourite destination but the one my mother was most often intent upon. She'd cruise past

French-style townhouses and blue-glassed high-rises and when we made it back to our studio, she'd fall into a deep quiet, the images of our sightseeing coiling in her gut until they choked her throat. I'd wake up to hear her crying in her sleep.

I didn't want one of those nights.

I told my mother I was hungry and she found a Taco Bell drive-thru. She parked in the lot and left the battery running so we could hear the radio as we ate.

"If I had a job I could buy you dinner sometimes," I said.

My mother stopped unwrapping her Taco Supreme. "You think you need to buy me dinner?"

"*Treat* you to dinner," I said. "I just meant that if I had a job—"

"How about you get a career in a few years and buy me a house instead," she said.

It always came back to school. Grades. The future. We never spoke about now.

My mother started eating, the corners of her mouth tightly drawn. Bits of chicken and sour cream dribbled onto her lap, and the takeout bag joined the others papered to the floor beneath my feet. She turned off the radio. But this wasn't the kind of silence I could settle in.

"I saw Nana today," I said, taking a bite from my burrito.

"You went over there?" She was working her mouth, biting the inside of her lip, like she was struggling between anger and something else. "How was it?"

"Tense. Quiet. They're not talking to each other."

She shrugged. "Figures."

"No, Mom, I mean they're messing with each other's heads."

When she asked me what I meant, I explained everything I'd seen. She nodded her head slowly as she used her tongue to dig out a shred of lettuce lodged in the grooves of her back teeth. "I see they've changed their methods since I was younger."

"They aren't yelling anymore."

"I guess they're too tired for that now."

"Doesn't that worry you?"

"Why would it?"

"I don't know, aren't you afraid that they'll kill each other or something?"

My mother chuckled and took another bite out of her taco. "I wouldn't worry. They hate each other too much to kill each other."

WE WERE WATCHING TV when a store manager called for me. Krissy from HMV. The voicemail picked up and she left a message asking me to come in for a group interview. I didn't turn to face my mother but stared straight ahead, focusing on the little girl with black hair in the Welch's Grape Juice commercial.

I wished Krissy would shut up. Her voice was chipper and did that thing my mother hated, that thing where everything she said sounded like a question. She left the store's contact information on the machine and finally ended the call. I let myself breathe a little but still didn't meet my mother's eyes.

"Anything you want to tell me?" she asked.

"It's just an interview."

"I said no, Kara. I told you the way it is."

"Yeah, but—"

"You should be focusing. You're this close to failing math. In two years you'll be applying for university. Think about that."

"But, Mom." I finally turned to look at her. "Don't you think a job could help with tuition? I mean, when the time comes."

"That will be handled," she said.

"Oh. Is there money put aside?"

The corner of my mother's eye twitched. "What are you saying?"

"Nothing. I was only asking."

The phone rang, though neither of us moved from our spots to answer it. I wasn't allowed to take calls on the house phone anyway, just in case a bill collector called and I didn't know which lie to tell them. It was a rule my mother hadn't lifted even when I became a teenager. The voicemail came on for a second time and after the beep all I heard was giggling. Gleeful. Somewhere just below manic.

It was Nana. She cackled about hiding my grandfather's books in the garage, someplace he'd never think to look; about making enough food for leftovers and keeping them in a mini-fridge she'd bought, one she kept in the bedroom. Bringing food out from the kitchen to anywhere else but the dining room was normally cause for Nana to yell and pace the hall for hours; the image of her hoarding pots of mackerel rundown and dumpling stew in her bedroom made me bite my fingernails.

"Since when do you bite your nails?"

"I don't really," I said.

"Then stop."

I put my hands in my lap and pressed my lips together. My mother shook her head at Nana's triumphant retellings and when the answering machine clicked off, she exhaled heavily. "She's definitely more creative now. I'll give her that," she said.

"This entire thing is insane," I said. "How are you not angry?"

"There are other things that deserve my anger more than this."

I didn't say anything. There was no point in staying on the subject. "You know, Yorkdale is only ten minutes away," I said quietly. "Fifteen if something happens on the subway."

"Kara, what did I say?"

I mumbled. "I just think it would be good for me."

My mother turned off the television. "You still have some reading to do or something, don't you?"

I got up from the sofa without a word and sat at the breakfast table in the kitchen. My copy of *Animal Farm* was on the other chair with my binder on top of it. Twenty minutes into reading, my mother interrupted me, shifting on the couch to look at me from across the room.

"Go to the interview and then we'll see," she said.

I paused. "Thanks, Mom."

"Why are you smiling at me?" she said. "Do your homework."

I WENT TO Nana's a week later; I didn't know what I expected to find. Every time they'd yelled at each other in the past, every time my grandfather had deserted the house to go back to his apartment, leaving with only the shoes he chose to walk out in, by the time I'd done a quick stop-by at Nana's, there he was, back on the couch.

This time, he was still in the living room, using the coffee table as a footrest, making an exhibition out of his moth-eaten socks — displaying them to the figurines, to the bungalow as a whole. The radio remained off, the loudest sound the *tick tick tick* of the clock, and the television wasn't even turned on to mute today. My grandfather had built himself a nest of newspapers and lottery tickets, once in a while singing to himself, "Oh yes, oh yes, I canna wait fi be paid and leave this wretched life behind!"

Nana was at the dining table. She had a teacup on one side of her, nestled in a saucer. On the other side, there was some bun and cheese on a plate. She was reading a bible aloud, leather-bound and gold-trimmed. It was my grandfather's. Nana's own bible, I knew, was small and weather-beaten; something my grandfather always mocked and something she always took pride in. "It just mean I read the Word more than yuh, nuh true?"

I stood in the archway between the foyer and living room, watching the two of them in their parallel universes connected by malicious pride. I wondered about the effort this took. I wanted to know what happened at night. Did my grandfather sleep in the bedroom next to Nana's? Did he go to the apartment he'd rented, only to come back in the morning? Or did they both just stay in their designated sections of the house? I wanted to ask but I was too angry to speak, too tired to unscramble a logic I didn't even want to understand.

Tick.

"Oh yes, oh yes, I canna wait fi be paid and leave this wretched life behind!"

Tick.

"'But I tell yuh say, that everyone will have fi give account on the day of judgement, Oh yes, fi every empty word they have spoken.' Matthew 12:36."

Tick.

I didn't take off my shoes before I rushed into the living room or look at either of my grandparents when I made it to the media cabinet. I seized the clock and threw it to the ground. No hesitation. I exhaled heavily when it crashed to the floor.

It should've smashed apart. The glass should've shattered into pieces. That was always what the movies showed. The dome was cracked; the gold frame of the clock was dented. At least it wouldn't work after this.

Nana had stood up. My grandfather hadn't abandoned his post on the couch but he stared at me with an alarmed fury. I was shaking.

"Sorry," I said. "I'm sorry." I was heading back toward the foyer. "I'll pay to have it fixed. Sorry." And I opened the front door, walking out of the house and down the sidewalk to the street before breaking into a run.

LOVELY

THE BOYFRIEND AND I DON'T SEE EACH OTHER much but when we do meet up it's at the theatre. Rochelle and Anita work concession, and I always tell my mother they're treating me to a free movie after work but it's been a while since I've gone to the SilverCity during one of their shifts.

The plan never changes. I slip into the theatre fifteen minutes before the boyfriend does and he finds me just before the lights go out, carrying a large bag of popcorn in one hand and a jumbo-sized Coke in the other. He used to grin and wave me away whenever I tried to hand him some cash for the snacks, but when he got home he'd discover a crinkled five-dollar bill tucked into the back of his shirt, some change in his back pocket. Now he accepts the money without any fuss but will find a way to give it back to me later, dropping the bills on the floor the next time we meet so I have no choice but to pick them up before someone else does.

I like the theatre, the comfort of the darkness and the intimacy of sitting next to the boyfriend, my hand on top of the armrest, his hand on top of mine, both of us facing the screen in front of us. Halfway through the movie, I always catch him staring at me with those kinda slick eyes — Anita calls them "or nah?" eyes — and sometimes I let him kiss me but pull away when he starts palming my shirt. Sometimes I eat my popcorn and act like I don't see him.

When we spoke last, the boyfriend said he wanted to do something other than see a movie.

"Girl, I just want to look at you. You know, face to face? Let's *go* somewhere."

It was three twenty on a Wednesday. He was waiting at the bus stop outside of his school and I was walking to the subway from mine. Our commute home is the only time I can talk to him and not just message him with the phone behind my back or halfway out of my pocket.

"Love, come on," he said.

The first few times he called me that, *Love*, I asked

him why — it's not like he's British or anything. When
he typed *becuz ur lovely* I rolled my eyes but didn't tell
him to stop. He whined for a few more minutes before
I agreed to have our next date somewhere else and my
knees trembled. My entire body felt like it would buckle
and that was what I just did — buckle to his will.

WE'RE SITTING IN the Burger King across the street from
the Eaton Centre now. The boyfriend gets a lot of attention. Girls standing in line glance back at us, bold yet
embarrassed, daring him to catch their gazes but blush-
ing at the possibility he might. He eats a bacon cheese-
burger with a boyish grin. Even the ketchup in the
corner of his mouth is kind of charming. He's not from
Toronto — he's a Brampton boy, a suburb kid — and for
this date, he's asked me to show him the places his high-
school field trips left out. But those places are all I really
know — my mother only recently moved us downtown,
after Graduate Housing accepted her application. Before
that, I'd just gone to high school in the city, five subway
stops away from the downtown core, and I'd always
stayed within the school's ten-block radius until it was
time to ride the northbound bus home.

I've taken the boyfriend to the different neighbourhoods my grade nine geography class explored when

Monsieur Wyatt made us do a scavenger hunt around the city. We've stopped here because the boyfriend needed to "refuel," and he wanted to sit by the window so he could see out to the crowds, to the Mormons handing out pamphlets and the shirtless Santa Claus drumming on upside-down buckets. His determination to be dazzled by his surroundings amuses me and irritates me at the same time. The way he acts as if a Burger King isn't pretty much the same no matter its location makes my eyes narrow, and I cross my arms over my chest, a deep groan pushing against my throat.

"You okay? You want me to get you something?"

He's sixteen, one year younger than me, and still asks those kinds of questions.

"I'm fine," I tell him. "You don't have to keep asking, you know."

I decide to end his tour with ice cream at the harbourfront forty-five minutes later. It feels like it's some kind of summer tradition in the city, the kind of thing he'll enjoy. When he messages me afterwards, to ask when we can see each other again, my mother is right next to me. I've left my braids in too long, they've become matted and frizzed, my natural hair knotted at the roots, and my mother is helping me comb out the tangles. My phone vibrates but I don't answer. My mother doesn't stop unravelling the braid she's been working on. She doesn't even look at me.

"Who's that?" she asks.

"A friend."

She doesn't respond right away and when she speaks, her voice is measured. "Hair's never stopped you from talking to Rochelle. Or Jordan."

I take a minute. I can always tell her me and Rochelle are fighting, which means I'm fighting with all of the girls in our group. It's not a total lie. Even when we'd just moved twenty minutes away to North York, I could only see the friends I had on Marlee Avenue on weekends; now that we've moved to a studio downtown I see them even less. But we still do talk. If I tell my mother I'm in an argument with them, she'll ask for details. I'll have to pretend to be sad or angry, keep my facts straight in my head. I'm rusty with active fibbing: I've graduated to simply keeping secrets. Still, no matter what, not saying anything feels easier than telling the truth.

Hannah and Justin, two people I hang out with in drama class, don't understand my secrecy at all.

"Kara, you're seventeen. At seventeen you can drive," said Justin. "You can move out of your mother's house, you can bartend —"

"That's nineteen," Hannah said.

"Actually, you can bartend at eighteen but the legal drinking age is nineteen," I said. "Ms. Janssen went over that in class."

"Whatever." Justin threw his hands in the air. "The point is, Kara, you're an adult. You're allowed to have a boyfriend."

I focus now on a knot at the end of my hair. *It's my boyfriend.* Maybe if I say it casually, like I expect her to be calm and not respond with homicidal rage. No, it won't work. That nonchalance is too Canadian. Too much like the kids I go to school with. Too white.

"It's a new friend," I say. "Rochelle's cousin."

That much is true. It's best to tell as much of the truth as I can.

"A cousin who's a boy." It's not a question.

"He was at Rochelle's birthday party a few months ago."

My mother picks up the comb and slices its tooth through my braid to uncoil it. "What did you two talk about?"

"Movies."

She combs through a knot, pulling apart the strands so that I gasp. "You've seen him since?" she asks.

"He lives in Brampton."

He told me once he didn't always have to be the

one to come down to where I lived, that I could visit
him too. Take the GO bus. We'd be at his house and
I wouldn't spend so much time scanning streets and
restaurants in fear of seeing someone my mother knew.
I don't know if I'm too scared to take up that offer or if
I don't think the risk is worth it.

"So you don't see him, then," says my mother.

"We usually just message each other," I say.

My mother doesn't say anything, and I'm quick
to fill the silence with my own voice. "So remember
that I have work tomorrow. I have morning shifts on
Saturdays."

"I'll drive you."

"It's okay," I say carefully. "I can get there myself."

WORK IS AT the HMV in Yorkdale Mall. I applied to be
a stock associate but they made me a cashier instead.
When we moved downtown, management offered to
transfer me to their Eaton Centre location but I enjoyed
the commute, enjoyed the time I had to myself on the
train, and I just told my mother there were no openings
in stores closer to us.

I'm quick at scanning and bagging but I never badger
the customers to take surveys, so I'm the first shift to be
cut during a slow Saturday morning. It's eleven thirty

and it'll take me half an hour to get back downtown, but there's no need to hurry home yet. My time is accounted for, and my mother won't call me for another five hours. I have the freedom of a full day.

The boyfriend lives an hour and a half away from the city—calling him down here seems like a waste of my time since we'd only get to spend about an hour together. I take out my phone to look at my contacts. I could reach out to Hannah and Justin—both of them can leave their houses easily—but I never talk to them outside of school; we aren't weekend kind of friends. I'm not too far away from the old neighbourhood. I can call Rochelle or Jordan, who'll text Anita and Aishani, and we can all go to Randy's for some patties or stop at the Wing Machine for a pound of Buffalo wings. But only if they answer their phones.

I default to the food court. It's not noon yet so I find a seat in the centre, beneath the domed ceiling, pretty quickly. Five bites into my pizza, I hear them. Natasha and Lisa, two girls who were hired with me from the group interview. I can see them out of the corner of my eye, only about two tables down from me, Lisa's purple braids clashing against her red shirt and Natasha's big gold hoop earrings tugging on her earlobes.

"Maybe we should ask her to sit with us," Natasha is saying.

"Why? It's not like she says anything more than 'hi' to us anyway."

"Maybe she's just quiet."

"Or maybe she's stush. Thinks she's too good to talk to us."

"Why you gotta be so loud? She'll hear you."

"So? You realize we know nothing about her, right? It's been, what, six months since we started working and we don't even know what school she goes to?"

My pizza is only half finished but I put the slice back into the paper bag and get up from my table, shouldering my green cross-body bag.

"See, she heard you!" Natasha whispered furiously. "Your mouth too loud!"

"I nuh care! I don't trust people who are that quiet. They're the ones who snap and shoot people up."

"If that's true," I say loudly, picking up my used napkins, "wouldn't the best course of action be to be nice to me so you don't become a target?"

It's the most I've ever said to them. I probably should have just ignored Lisa — she's like Anita, always has to be the loudest one in the room — and left quietly to eat my pizza on the train while I thought of something to do other than go back to the apartment. But I wanted to stun them into silence, let them see a side of me I wanted them to see. On my way to the escalator I can hear Lisa shouting, "See? She's a fucking psycho!"

One time the boyfriend told me he didn't really know me. Each time we see a movie, we stay in the theatre even after the credits finish rolling, cushioned in our seats until the cleanup crew kicks us out. That night they didn't come for a while, so we were able to stay longer than usual, and the boyfriend reached over the armrest to stroke a strand of hair away from my face.

"We can go somewhere after this," he said. "Tell your mom the subway's down or something, give us some more time."

"Go somewhere and do what?"

"Talk. Whatever."

I raised my eyebrows. "I thought boys didn't like girls who talked too much."

The boyfriend laughed. "You don't talk at all, love. Not about, I don't know, real things."

"That's specific."

"Don't do that," he said. When I opened my mouth he shook his head. "And don't pretend like you don't know you're doing it."

"I don't know what you mean by real things. Be specific."

He shrugged his shoulders and scratched the little stubble he had on his chin. "School. Parent stuff. I don't know, *things*. The things I tell you."

I held up my index finger. "One, school's hard." Then my middle finger, so I was making the peace sign. "Two, my mom is . . . she's my mom." My fourth finger. "Three, was there a number three?"

"What about your dad?" he asked.

"What about him?"

"He isn't around, right?"

I stared at the black screen. Two guys with brooms and dustpans ambled into the theatre. One of them shouted, "Movie's over, guys!"

"Yeah, movie's over," said the other. "You don't have to go home but you can't stay here!"

The boyfriend got up first and dropped a twenty-dollar bill on the floor, his way of refusing my payment for the movie tickets. I picked it up without a word because I'd already stuffed a twenty-dollar bill in his gym bag when he went to the washroom, anticipating this move.

I MET THE boyfriend at Rochelle's eighteenth birthday. The party started at seven, and my mother was going to pick me up at ten even though no one else would even show up until at least eight thirty. When I got to Rochelle's, her mother, Ms. B, was still bustling around the kitchen, cooking what smelled like jerk chicken, and Rochelle was hanging up streamers in the basement, standing on top of the ripped leather couch to reach the ceiling. She wasn't even dressed yet, wearing grey lounge shorts and a tattered shirt with the Jamaican flag splayed across the chest.

"Hold the other side nuh," she said.

I climbed onto the sofa and balanced myself on the frame, taping the other end of the streamer against the wall. Rochelle suddenly got irritated.

"Ay, are you going to set up the stereo or just stare at my friend's batty all day?"

"Damn, Chelle, why you gotta be like that?"

I hadn't noticed there was someone else in the basement with us. The boyfriend was crouched in a corner by the entrance, bent in front of a large speaker. I glanced away as soon as I spotted him. I couldn't stare at cute boys for too long.

"That's just my Brampton cousin," Rochelle told me. "He's a *Star Wars* geek."

"*Chelle!*"

"Oh." I stepped off the couch and followed Rochelle back upstairs. "I like *Lord of the Rings* better."

At eight o'clock another three people showed up: a guy in a du-rag and two girls in jersey dresses, one of them sporting the Lakers and the other one the Sixers. Anita, Aishani, and Jordan probably wouldn't come until my mom picked me up at ten; they always tried to be the latest ones to anything. We stayed upstairs — there weren't enough people for the basement to become the place to be yet. Rochelle and the other girls skipped to her bedroom to find her something to wear, and I sat down in the living room since I wouldn't be of any help. I'd come in basics: blue jeans and a fitted camouflage shirt. I never spent more than ten minutes deciding what to wear.

Ms. B had finished most of the cooking, and the dining table was crowded with aluminum trays stuffed with rice and peas, jerk chicken, potato salad, curry goat. We weren't supposed to start eating until at least another ten people showed up, but the boyfriend crept around the kitchen and snatched a couple of fried dumplings from a pan on the stove, keeping a lookout for Ms. B, who'd gone to the bathroom. He handed me a dumpling as he sat next to me on the floral living room sofa.

Du-rag watched us from the armchair. "Wow, you couldn't get me any?"

"I only got two hands, don't I?"

"Oh I see," he said, grinning. "This is one of your moves, right? Being all chivalrous and shit."

"Whatever."

I stared at the dumpling. "Thanks." The truth is, I don't like fried dumplings. I prefer them boiled and mixed in stew with yams and chicken, a preference that everyone tells me is weird.

"You're wrong, you know," said the boyfriend. "About *Star Wars*."

"You heard that?"

He grinned. "Yeah, I heard that."

The house started getting packed around eight forty-five, and there was an unspoken system to the party: take your shoes off at the door, pack your paper plate with food, thank Ms. B, and then beeline to the basement where the music was, where the dance floor was, where Rochelle was. Even downstairs, I sat on the tattered couch and watched the party ebb and flow in front of me. Rochelle danced in the centre of the basement, the gold belly chain circled around her midriff glinting in the dark and hypnotizing the guys posted up against the wall. The boyfriend found me and sat next to me again—even though when he'd sat next to me upstairs, we'd just talked about movies; even though for each group of girls that passed by us, one of them would ask him to dance.

"Look, I don't dance," I said. "So if you want to try to catch a bubble or something, feel free to talk to one of those girls."

"Don't worry, love," he said. "I don't dance either."

It was a lie, a corny one, and it almost made me smile.

The next day Rochelle messaged me to tell me he'd asked for my number and she'd given it to him.

He likes u. Deal wit it.

MY MOTHER'S HAVING one of her restless nights, where she needs to be free of our studio or else ends up in a sour mood, yelling about the size of the apartment and her shitty boss, about my failing math grade, about life. She asks me to keep her company when she goes driving, choosing to take the highway to the Woodbridge suburbs, and while she's concentrating on passing a slow-moving Prius I ask her how she met my dad.

"What?"

I've only asked her this once before, when I was thirteen, and she pretended not to hear me.

Her hands grip the steering wheel. "Why are you asking about that?"

"I don't know," I say, because it's true.

"There are no letters, you know," she says. "No emails I've deleted or messages I've kept from you. He asks about you if I ever have to call and beg him for the child support he was supposed to pay years ago and I tell you when he does. Minimal effort, Kara."

She's getting angry.

"I was just curious, Mom," I say.

"For no reason whatsoever?"

I press my lips together.

"*Well?*"

"You two meeting, it's kind of like my origin story, that's all."

"Your 'origin story'?"

"Yeah," I say. "Isn't it?"

There's a beat before my mother speaks again. "My friend liked him," she says. "She asked me to tell him that and he told me he liked me instead. I should've known from then."

"And then what happened?"

She shrugs. "We dated."

I wait, but she doesn't say anything else. "That's it?"

"Yes."

"But —"

"You asked me how we met and I told you, end of story. If you're that interested, why don't you call him and ask him yourself?"

I'm not going to do that and she knows it too. I have no resentments I need him to hear or explanations I need him to give. I don't carry him with me like she does, and she's always felt like I've betrayed her because of it.

"I was just curious," I say again.

"Yeah, well," my mother switches on her turning signal and glides into the next lane. "Didn't curiosity kill the cat?"

THE BOYFRIEND'S HOUSE is nice. He's polite and gives me a tour of the living room with its old-fashioned fireplace and of the kitchen with its granite countertops. It's the kind of house my mother would like. Framed family photos nailed to the wall guide us up the stairs to the second floor and there, the boyfriend invites me into his bedroom. It's messy but not a mess. An empty white hamper. A pile of clothes on a swivel chair. A cedar wood desk and translucent blue iMac. He has a tube TV on top of his dresser, hooked up to a portable DVD player and Xbox.

It took me a month to finally make it here, to want to see where he lives.

We sit on his twin bed to watch *The Chamber of Secrets*, and the boyfriend's mouth is on mine even before the flying Ford Anglia appears. He holds nothing back and shifts to lay me down, brushing my tank top upward. I feel the mechanics of his touch, of his hands on my skin, on my waist, on my breasts, all the things that are supposed to make me ache. Wet splotches smack against my neck, and I'm reminded of my first kiss with the first boy I ever made out with. Terrence Peters. I didn't feel much of anything then, either. I wonder if I can, if I ever will. The TV is still visible from my position, and I catch Uncle Vernon falling into the rosebushes as Harry escapes.

The boyfriend whispers in my ear. "I have condoms."

"Okay."

I'm not nervous. Or scared. I just want to know. I want to know if I can feel anything, if he can discover me, open me up. He said he wanted to know me; maybe he meant that I never give anything of myself over to him. He kisses me again, and I push myself to react, to wrap my arms around him and crush him to me.

When it's over, I'm still looking at the tubed screen. Harry can't use Floo Powder properly and ends up in Knockturn Alley. The boyfriend's lying on his front, his face buried in a pillow, and he puts his arm across my middle, half-awake and half-asleep. "You okay, love?" He turns his head to look at me. "How do you feel?"

Unchanged and unmoved. I don't know if that's a good thing or a bad thing and I just keep watching the movie.

"Fine," I say. "I feel fine."

FAITH COMMUNITY

WE'D BEEN PARKED IN THE SUN FOR OVER AN hour when Nana strutted out of the entrance of Faith Community Baptist Church with the other churchgoers. My grandfather was at her back, walking as if he were being pulled along by an invisible string. His arms swung lazily at his sides as he followed Nana's quick steps across the church's parking lot to the sidewalk.

We were in a private lot across the street. I nudged my mother awake, took my feet off of the glove compartment and put them back into my buckle-up sandals. My mother eased the driver's seat into its original position and pulled out her messy ponytail. She wiped her forehead as she gathered her hair in her palms, but the sweat had already begun to naturalize the strands: she could only manage to put her hair up in a puffy bun. I looked out the window. With every two steps, Nana stopped to grab hands with her Brothers and Sisters, and to, I was sure, Bless them with God's Good Fortune. My grandfather stayed behind her like always, his closed-lip smile failing to prevent interaction and in fact encouraging it. Bible-holding men in brown suits and women in loud purple, blue, or red dresses huddled around him like seagulls. Quiet and distant, my grandfather was a challenge—and so naturally attracted the meddlesome interest of the flock.

He and Nana started walking across the street toward us, and I could hear them out of the rolled-down windows, Nana's voice snapping the air like a firecracker.

"I canna believe how yuh embarrass me, suh! Canna even wear a suit! Canna even talk to the people them, canna even—"

"Hush up, woman! I shaved, I woke up early, and I came. That's all you're getting from me."

"Oh so the Lawd nuh worthy of anything else, eh? Yuh canna be nice for five minutes? Yuh canna—"

"All you do is talk, you know? Just chat, chat, chat, chat, chat, pick, pick, pick, pick, pick. I can't wait to die just to get away from your wretched mouth."

"Yuh a terrible man, George Davis. What sin must me have commit fi be stuck with a man so hateful? I—"

My mother and I rolled up the windows and turned on the air conditioner. By the time they crossed over to the parking lot, we had reapplied lipstick and lip gloss, laid a towel down on the back seat to cover up the coffee stains, and turned the radio from Flow 93.5 to 680 News. It was the only station that was suitable for Nana's Christian ears but didn't make me and my mother want to bang our heads against the dashboard.

Nana reached the car, but my grandfather stopped walking a few feet away. He dug into his pocket and took out a cellphone—he still had the kind that flipped up—pressing a finger to his free ear to better hear whoever was speaking.

"Hi, Nana," I said as she climbed into the back seat.

"Yes, hi, Kara." She fidgeted over the towel, straightened out the front of her dress with her gloved hands, finally sat still, and then started shifting her weight again. "Why do I haffi sit on this towel here, suh? Yuh canna shampoo yuh car?"

"When you called this morning you said service would be done at noon. It's one thirty," said my mother.

"Yuh nuh know how the Spirit move, Eloise," said Nana. "When it take hold of yuh, yuh nuh walk away from it. Yuh nuh know about these things."

My mother closed her eyes the way she did whenever she regretted reconnecting with her parents. We were only here today because my grandfather had nearly died six months ago, and it had been too near a tragedy for my mother and me to ignore. But the near-frequent contact with them was wearing at us.

My mother tapped her fingers on the steering wheel. "Who is George talking to?"

Nana kissed her teeth but didn't answer.

"Go get your grandfather, Kara."

I sighed and got out of the car and when I approached my grandfather, he put the phone behind his back.

"What you want, pickney?"

He still called me that, even though I was seventeen and a long way away from being a child. The only time he'd ever addressed me by name was the day I graduated high school.

"We're all waiting for you," I said.

"Just hold on, nuh. I'll be there in a minute."

"Who're you talking to?"

"That's none of your business," he said. "Just g'way! Go on!"

Nana was staring at us through the window, her lips pursed, her eyebrows creased, her entire face a slow collapse into resignation. I looked back toward my grandfather. He'd moved several feet away and turned his back, the phone to his ear. I crept closer until I could make out what he was saying.

"Lorraine," he whispered.

"So?" my mother said when I got back into the passenger's seat. I looked at her pointedly. "He might be a while, I don't know."

The way she set her mouth let me know she understood. She rolled down her window again and pushed the heel of her palm against the horn for one loud blare. "Let's go, George!"

"Eloise," said Nana, "Yuh nuh haffi make so much noise!"

"*Now*, George!"

His expression was one of lazy defiance as he hung up and ambled over to our car. "Just gwaan without me. I have my car at a body shop around here and it fix up. I'm going to pick it up."

"Then you can drive Nana home," said my mother.

"My car too messy for her and mi nuh want fi hear her mouth. It might be a while before it ready to drive out too."

"Nah want him fi drive me anyway, him drive like a madman, like one of them Chiney."

"Nana," I said, turning to her. "You know you can't say stuff like that."

She kissed her teeth for a second time, and my

mother rolled her eyes and groaned, picking at the back end of her bun.

"Eloise, yuh know yuh mustn't fi pick at yuh head," said Nana. I could feel her lean forward in the back seat to examine my mother's head more closely. "Eh-eh, it sweat out! This how yuh go fi work? With the white people them?"

"I didn't wait out in this hot car for over an hour just for you to criticize me, Verna," said my mother.

"Eloise, me only just say—"

The need to get out of the car suddenly over-whelmed me. Staying for the drive would only mean navigating the spoken and unspoken bickering between Nana and my mother; I already knew that spending time with my grandfather wouldn't stress me out nearly as much.

"I'll go with you, Grandpa," I said. "You can drop me off at Nana's when you're done if it's easier."

He pursed his lips but my mother stopped him before he could begin to protest. "You don't want to spend time with your granddaughter, George?"

"A'right, fine—but mi nuh gwine fi slow down for yuh, yuh hear? Yuh best walk up fast." He was annoyed. That was the only time his accent really came out, full-blown and unrestrained. I got out of the car and smiled.

"Call me if anything goes wrong," said my mother,

shifting into gear. I took one last look at Nana, who waved goodbye but kept her face toward the driver's seat.

DESPITE HIS WARNING, my grandfather kept a leisurely pace and we walked to the main road in silence. That was nothing new — what little time we spent alone together was nearly always passed reading in his bedroom at Nana's house, the door closed to her clattering in the kitchen. Sometimes he'd put on a record, Prince Buster or the Skatalites, and we'd bob our heads to it in unison. The quiet between us now allowed me to breathe and feel settled and I hated myself for how easy it was for me to be in his company.

"I won't go into her house," I said. "I'll say hello at the door but I'm not going inside."

"Fine."

"So you are going to a woman's house, then."

"I nuh say that."

"Then what are you saying?"

"Nothing. You're the one saying something."

I wanted to punch him. He knew it too. There was a kind of jaunt to his step now, the same one he had whenever he walked away from Nana after eliciting an indignant yell from her. Like he felt pleased whenever he frustrated us. It had taken three different sleepovers at three different houses for me to realize that not all families worked this way.

"I don't even know how you and Nana met. Neither of you talk about it."

"Nothing to say."

"Of course there is. Grandparents are supposed to tell their grandchildren how they met."

"A'right. It was 1966. She was a pretty likkle school-girl and I called to her and she came."

"That can't be it. That's not how people meet."

"It's how men and women meet."

"No it isn't, you're just being difficult."

"You don't see the boys them calling out to the girls them on the street? They don't call out to you?"

"Not really, no."

"You're lucky then."

I scowled. We were almost at the main road, Lawrence Avenue, a busy street for traffic but a lonely one for walking—all of civilization was at the strip mall with the Tim Hortons and the big-box Walmart, or else inside the grey apartment buildings that stood, washed-out and faded, beside the sidewalk.

He reached into his pocket for a packet of gum and offered me a stick of Juicy Fruit. I'd told him once, years ago, that it was my favourite brand and that was all he carried since then, wordlessly offering me a piece

whenever we were around each other. I took it and sav-
oured the sweetness only for a moment; accepting any
offer from him felt like condoning his bad behaviour, a
betrayal to Nana and my mother, and he had to know
I was on their side. I spit the gum out.

"Did you and Nana always hate each other or did
that just come with age?"

"Mi nuh hate nobody. Just want fi be left alone. Just
want some peace."

He carefully peeled off the silver wrapper from a
stick of gum. The action seemed sad. Everything he did
seemed sad, all of his movements, all of his gestures.
Even the way the corner of his lips drooped, pulling
down his already-long face, cloaked his features in a
melancholy I couldn't pinpoint. When I was younger,
I thought everything he did was angry. I'd been afraid
of him as a child: every time he decided to stop by
Nana's, whether it was for a day or a few weeks at a
time, it seemed like he wanted to feel the house shrink
in his presence. I would never get caught around him
without Nana present because of that. The first time
I was alone with him had been when he took me to
Clarinda's — and it hadn't been a planned trip.

My mother had charged Nana with taking care of me
for the day, but the nursing home called Nana into work
for an emergency and I was left in my grandfather's

care. I'd sat on the living room carpet, my back against the plastic-covered sofa, and watched as she rushed from her bedroom to the kitchen.

After she'd left, the screen door banging against the frame, I stayed where I was, the TV my only company. It wasn't long before I heard the bedroom door creak open and felt the floorboards sink beneath footsteps—heavy and slow. My grandfather appeared in the archway that separated the living room from the hallway.

"Come with me," he'd said.

"Where are we going?"

"It doesn't matter where we're going, you're coming."

"Nana said to stay in the house."

"Well, I'm saying we're leaving for a while."

I stared at the TV. I didn't know him. I didn't recognize his authority. "Mom said to do what Nana tells me to do."

"Yuh mother nuh tell yuh sey yuh haffi respect yuh elders? I'm your grandfather, you listen to me. Let's go!"

His car was parked at the bottom of the driveway, its rear jutting out over the sidewalk. Newspapers and screwdrivers and parts of old record players and old televisions littered the back seat, so I had to sit up front with him.

"You like ska?"

I shrugged.

"Probably never even heard ska." He pushed a tape into the deck, and I jolted at the abrupt loudness of the trumpets.

"Derrick Morgan."

The jaunty sway of the piano and guitar encouraged me to bounce in my seat, and my grandfather chuckled as he mimicked my movements. I grinned back and asked him to rewind the tape to the same song.

"What grade you in?"

"Grade four."

"You like it?"

"I hate math." I looked at him. I knew nothing about him but he still felt lonely to me, like maybe he didn't talk much because nobody ever asked him to. "Did you like grade four?" I said.

"I was starting to work then so I didn't go to school much." He glanced at me and, seeing my expression, he cleared his throat. "Things were different in Jamaica back then."

It hadn't been too long before he'd pulled up in front of a hair salon. *Black Beauty Hair Shop* was printed large, pink and swirly on the plate-glass display window. Clarinda was already standing outside the store, wearing a red sundress made from a sheer material that incited in me the urge to rip and tear, to feel the fabric pull apart in my hands. Later I remembered the visit only in snatches—the way his voice smoothed out to a slyness I hadn't heard before, the way Clarinda led him upstairs to her apartment—but the dress had been emblazoned on my mind and I couldn't stop describing it to my mother when she picked me up at the end of the day. She yelled for details about Clarinda's appearance, but I could only tell her that the colour of the dress had hurt my eyes.

PICKING UP THE car only took ten minutes when I'd thought it would take at least twenty. The repair shop owner, Oliver, was a friend of my grandfather's, and I bit my tongue when he squeezed my cheeks between his thumb and forefinger. I was old enough to drink, smoke, and vote but apparently looked young enough to pinch. I tried not to seethe.

"This likkle skinny gyal here is mi grand-pickney."

"Oh yes," said Oliver, looking at me as he wiped his hands with an oily rag. "The one who does the film t'ing, nuh true?"

"Why?" I said. "Has George introduced you to other grandkids?"

My grandfather looked at me like he wanted to slap some respect into me, but Oliver laughed and I

laughed with him. We left in the car, a faded blue jal-
opy, and instead of driving down Lawrence to Marlee,
my grandfather turned onto a side street and parked
in front of a house with a small veranda and paper
blinds covering the windows, plastic plants and silk
flowers lining the sill.

He reached behind my seat and picked up a red tool-
box. "Nuh go anywhere," he said. He got out of the car
and walked up the driveway to the house.

I watched as he rang the doorbell and waited. The
woman who answered was tall and curvy and not
young but younger. She ushered him inside and a knot
choked my throat when the door shut behind them.

The situation was strange in how familiar it was. My
grandfather had loved women even when I was a child,
even before I'd been born, and the only consequence of
his infidelities had been an eventual residential separation. But he'd still had a key to Nana's house, still had a
room, the security of a waiting meal. The apartment he
rented was more like a backup plan for when their arguing got too much for him to handle. The separation was
part-time and loosely enforced. Both he and Nana kept
right on wearing their wedding bands like they meant
something, even though it looked to me that being in
each other's company only seemed to exhaust one and
enrage the other. I'd allowed myself to reconsider my

opinion when they decided to renew their vows three months ago, after my grandfather had survived the car accident and realized what was important in life.

I used to think Nana didn't know about the other women, but that changed when we went to the market one day when I was eleven. Too busy judging the mangoes with her sniffs and with her squeezes, she hadn't noticed the woman by the oranges, looking at her from the side of her eye.

At fifty, Nana hadn't succumbed her style to age or modernity yet. She'd still cut and cropped her hair into soft curls and sashayed out in swing dresses, like something out of a Dorothy Dandridge movie. I'd gotten used to seeing women of all ages glare at her. I thought that was all this was, too—until the woman walked up to us, a kind of vindictive determination in her step.

"Excuse me," she'd said. "Do we know each other? I feel like we do."

Nana had turned away from the fruit to look at the woman, her eyes doing their habitual up-down. The woman was pretty, younger than Nana by at least a few years. Her skin was smooth and dark, and her voice was punctuated by an accent I couldn't put my finger on—neither Jamaican nor Trinidadian, but some other island.

"A what church yuh go?"

"Reverend Mitchell's church," the woman said. "Christ Temple Pentecostal?"

"Never heard of it."

"Must be something else then."

"Nuh worry, it will come to me."

I looked from Nana to the woman and back again. I watched as a smile twisted Nana's face, watched her stand up a little taller, raise her neck a little higher. "Yuh must be a friend of George," she said. "Him a man with lots of friends."

"Must be it. He's helped me out a lot, George."

"Yes, him a giving man." Nana put her hand on my shoulder and pulled me to her side. "Him ever show yuh this likkle bright-eye gyal here? Our likkle granddaughter. Kara say 'hi' to this nice lady."

The woman flicked her eyes downward to me. "Pretty girl." She looked back up at Nana and smiled. "Well, I have a lot of errands to run. I just wanted to say hello."

"All right. God bless yuh now."

The woman nodded once, then walked down the aisle to the cash registers, and Nana went back to inspecting fruit, picking up and putting down mangoes, the corners of her mouth taut. I wanted to touch her, put my hand on her back, but thought about how my mother pushed me away whenever I tried that with her.

So I just held open the clear, plastic bag for when Nana needed to put away some plums or peaches.

She was silent on the walk back to her house, and I skipped alongside her, kicking up stones with my shoes, doing what I could to let her know that I'd found nothing strange about the woman in the marketplace. We made it to her driveway right when my mother pulled up behind my grandfather's car, which was parked at the bottom. I stared at his licence plate and wondered if Nana would ban him from her house.

There was a honk and I said bye to Nana, who looked at my mother in farewell, and got into the Buick.

"Put on your seat belt," said my mother as she drove off. I did what she said and then kept my head turned to the side, looking out the window.

"You're quiet today," said my mother. "You usually have a few things to say to me when you come back from Nana's."

I started twirling my fingers around each other. "Do you think they're lonely?"

"Who?"

"Nana and Grandpa. Do you think they're lonely?"

"Why?"

"I don't know."

My mother slowed down to a stop at a red traffic light. "Nana probably is, yeah," she said.

"What about you? Are you lonely?"

She turned to me and curled her thumb and fore-finger under my chin. The light turned green again, and she continued driving.

IT WASN'T LONG before my grandfather got back into the car, his appearance the same as it was before, everything the same as it was before, like he hadn't spent twenty minutes in some woman's house. It infuriated me, how easy it was for him to continue on like nothing happened, and I kept my face to the window as he drove, following the passing trees and muddy-brown apartment complexes with my eyes. He turned on the radio to some jazz, a tickle in my throat and a flutter in my chest, and I turned it back off. He grumbled but didn't do anything else.

"I don't understand you," I said finally.

"That's okay," he said. "I nuh need yuh fi understand me."

At Nana's house, my mother's car took up the driveway, and my grandfather had to settle for the street. Inside it smelled like oxtail and rice, salty and rich. The TV was on, the volume loud enough to overpower the religious mutterings coming from the stereo. My mother was sitting on the couch, her ponytail even more dishevelled, her face stiff with irritation. My grandfather unlaced his shoes in the foyer, and Nana walked toward him and watched him take them off.

"Last time I leave my shoes here, I found candy wrappers in them," he said.

"I tell you say, if you take a candy from my likkle bowl there, fi throw the wrapper inna the garbage but yuh nuh listen, yuh put the wrapper back inna the bowl."

My grandfather kissed his teeth but his expression was soft, his body loose. "Oxtail smell burnt," he said.

Nana laughed and waved her hand dismissively. She headed back to the kitchen. "My oxtail never burn, I cook it nice all the time."

I pushed my sandals onto the shoe mat against the wall and watched as my grandfather took a seat at the middle of the plastic-covered table, Nana taking the lid off of her dutchie pot to see how much rice was left. He interlocked his fingers on the table, a look of satisfied anticipation on his face.

My mother called to me.

She turned down the volume of the TV when I joined her on the sofa and she looked at me expectantly. "Well," she said. "What happened? Where'd you go? Nana would not shut up for the two hours you were gone."

Even before opening my mouth I realized that I'd known from the moment my grandfather had pulled up to Lorraine's house that I wasn't going to say anything about the visit, that I didn't want the house to echo with screams so loud they'd wrack my entire body. My grandfather had known it, too—my mother made scenes; I didn't—and I forced myself to swallow the bitter humiliation of being so predictable in my need for quiet.

"We went to the shop. It took longer than expected."

I could tell she knew I was lying but she didn't ask me any more questions, she only turned the volume back up on the TV. She had to know what I'd only just now discovered: that peace could only exist in this family when we lied about everything, at least to each other.

Inside the dining room, Nana was gliding from the fridge to the cupboards to the stove, taking out drinks and plates and forks, moving like a type of dance. My grandfather watched her movements, smiling slightly, his eyes tracing the outline of her figure, and I told myself not to stare at them too long because if he caught me, he would remember himself and his smile would vanish.

CELEBRATION

THEY GOT DRUNK TOGETHER FOR THE FIRST time — a bottle of sparkling wine the culprit — on Kara's eighteenth birthday. Both women, short and tiny, were pretty much gone after the third glass, and on the fourth, Eloise swallowed hard and tapped her finger ruefully on the dining table.

"It's not because you're eighteen," she said, stifling a burp. "It's because you're graduating."

Kara thought it looked like her mother was about to say something else but after a short pause, Eloise guzzled down the last of her drink and poured herself another glass instead.

Kara took another sip and thought back to her last birthday, when Eloise had dropped her off at the subway so she could take the train downtown to school. She'd opened the car door to leave but Eloise had grabbed her by the wrist, pulling her back into the passenger's seat.

"I just want you to imagine something," she'd said. "I was your age when you were born."

Kara had only blinked twice at her, slack-jawed and silent, and then Eloise told her to have a good day. Every few months after that, she'd pipe up and say to Kara, "When I was your age, you were three months . . . six months . . . nine months . . . fat and crying and hungry. Can you imagine that? Can you imagine dealing with that?"

But none of those questions were asked this time. Eloise had come home early, a bottle of Prosecco in hand, and told Kara to get two glasses from the kitchen cupboard. Kara had another year until she was legal but they were going to celebrate anyway. She was about to be a high-school graduate and she had offers, possibilities, from a full ride to York University to a "Congratulations!" letter from the University of Toronto, an acceptance she'd been working toward since her first year of high school.

They raised their glasses for a fifth toast and after their rims clinked together Eloise started to giggle, the

throaty cackle bouncing off all the walls of the living
room, of the entire bachelor.

DRUNK

1.

The lunch period was halfway finished when Justin and Hannah each received a call. For Hannah it was her mother; for Justin it was the housekeeper. Apparently the mail had come to both houses and they each had envelopes addressed to them.

"Well, is it big or small?" said Justin.

Hannah twirled her blonde hair around her finger. "Is it thick? Yes, open it."

I'd already gotten my envelopes, all three of them thick with "Congratulations!" letters and course catalogues. My mother and I had a pros and cons list taped to the fridge, and I'd done the friend freak-out with

Rochelle, the one person from my old neighbourhood who still talked to me, the one person who knew I didn't think I was too stush for Eglinton West and Marlee now.

Rochelle was going to go to University of Toronto, the Mississauga campus, and she'd informed me that Anita was choosing Sheridan. Anita had been the first to brush me off whenever I found myself back in the neighbourhood. Then, not too long after Anita stopped coming to meet me, Aishani would always be working whenever I came by, and Jordan would just be "busy." Rochelle told me Jordan had decided on York, and Aishani was struggling with whether she wanted to go to university at all—the student loans would bury her and she didn't want to spend the rest of her life owing back.

Justin got off the phone first and then Hannah. Dalhousie had accepted Hannah and Queen's had rejected Justin. He jumped down from the tree he'd climbed the minute we got to the park and walked over to the chain-link fence Hannah was leaning against. I stayed sitting at the base of another tree not too far away, balancing myself on my knapsack so my jeans wouldn't be grass-stained.

"The suicide rate up there is insane anyway." Justin reached into his cargo shorts for a pack of menthols. "I'm better off going to McMaster."

"You got off the waiting list?" said Hannah.

He cupped his hand around a blue lighter as he sparked his cigarette, then took a drag before answering her. "It's only a matter of time," he said, scratching the mole on his right cheek. Smoke billowed from his mouth, and I scrunched up my nose to keep from inhaling anything.

Hannah snorted. "You're pretty sure of yourself."

"No reason not to be," said Justin with a shrug and a grin.

His easy confidence wasn't for show and it burned me. I didn't know how to be that relaxed; it came across as arrogant. But still, it had to be nice.

"Well, I want to celebrate," said Hannah. "I heard a few people are ditching the afternoon, going to Andrei's."

"Oh yeah?" Justin leaned over the fence and spat into someone's backyard. "Which people?"

"Nora, Ryan, Sebastian. Maybe a few others."

"Sweet."

I didn't say anything. Those people were just faces I saw in the hall; I knew none of them. I didn't really know Hannah and Justin, either. For the first two years of high school I'd only hung out with Terrence Peters. But when his family moved to Whitby, I somehow found myself with Justin and Hannah. I was in the same drama class as them and had been since the beginning of high school. We were always the stronger actors, and a lot of the time we were put together for group projects. At the beginning of last year, Hannah asked if I wanted to spend lunch with them. It became routine before I really knew what was happening.

"So Kara, how about it?" said Justin.

I pushed my lips to the side, as if I were considering the option. "I'll pass, thanks."

"What is your, like, beef or whatever with fun?" said Hannah.

"My 'beef'?"

"I'm serious, you've gotten into all of your dream schools, what's the point of even going to class anymore?"

"Hannah, the last time I skipped school it didn't exactly go well," I said.

"You really need to let that go. It was, like, a million years ago, and we won't ditch you like they did, I promise."

"If I leave now I think I might be able to grab something to eat before French."

"Be serious. Do you really want to spend the afternoon doing conjugations in French class?" said Hannah. "It's Friday!"

"I don't, but —"

"Don't you get it? None of your schools rejected you," said Justin. "You can do whatever the hell you want. Seize the fucking day, man."

When I only blinked at them, Hannah groaned and pretended to choke me. "Your mom won't find out, okay? She isn't God."

Justin started looking to his left then to his right and back again. He looked up to the sky, moving his head in frantic circles as if waiting for something to fall. "Hannah dared to blaspheme against Kara's mom and wasn't struck down by lightning?" He gasped. "What is this miracle?"

"Stop it," I said. "You're not funny."

"I'm a little funny."

"You're a jackass," said Hannah. She turned to me. "You've kept a secret boyfriend from your mom, you can skip an afternoon. Let's go."

She took my arm and started pulling me up from the grass. They were so sure I was entitled to a little bit of mayhem.

"I don't even know Andrei," I said.

"That doesn't matter, you're with us," said Hannah. She turned to Justin. "Right?"

He nodded. "Yep. You're with us."

2.

Andrei's father answered the front door. He was a tall man — so tall he hunched. His hair was greying and his face was thin and drawn, his pale skin tight to his bones. He was bundled in a red terry cloth robe and had on gym socks even though he was wearing brown slippers. I took a step backward, preparing to turn on my heel and run away, but Justin smiled.

"Hey, Mr. K," he said.

"Justin!"

Mr. K clapped Justin on the shoulder, quizzing him about girls and grades like he was a proud uncle. He then turned to Hannah and chuckled before pulling her diminutive body into a tight hug. When he finally saw me, he stared.

"This is Kara," said Justin. "A friend."

Andrei's father nodded and stepped to the side to let us through. "Andrei is at the back."

The house wasn't a mansion but it was close enough to one that I had to remind myself to appear unmoved. I didn't want the amazement to show on my face as I followed Justin and Hannah through a foyer that could probably hold my grandmother's entire bungalow. I looked behind me, expecting Mr. K to be trailing our footsteps, but he was walking up a spiral staircase to the next floor of the house.

The back turned out to be the living room. It was spacious and sparse in that modern kind of way: grey suede couches and beige carpeting, a television that took up nearly the entire wall. Andrei was standing at a stocked bar, pulling his brown hair into a bun. Ryan Collingwood sat on the sofa, still wearing his school-issued gym shorts. On the coffee table in front of him were two glasses nestled on coasters and a small bag of weed. Hannah and Justin walked over to the couches but I stayed where I was. I'd expected us to hang out in the basement or in Andrei's room; the openness of the living room made me anxious.

"What's her deal?" said Ryan, nodding his head toward me.

Hannah put her feet up on the couch and watched as he started to roll a joint. "She's shy. You guys know Kara, right? Kara . . ." — she looked at me — "Davis?"

I nodded.

"Kara Davis," said Hannah again.

"Yeah, sure," said Andrei. He gestured to the liquor bottles on the bar. "What's your drink, Kara Davis?"

Justin laughed. "She doesn't drink."

"You don't know that," I said. I'd spoken before thinking, but I didn't take it back. I didn't like being predictable; it felt too much like a weakness.

Hannah grinned at me from the couch. "She'll have what I'm drinking," she said. "A screwdriver."

Andrei snapped his fingers. "Got it." He glanced at me. "You know, you can sit down. You're making me nervous standing there like that."

The armchair was nearest. I was comforted slightly by being closest to the front door.

"Where is everyone? I thought Nora was coming," said Justin.

"Dude, my bed is off limits," said Andrei.

Justin leaned back onto the couch. "Whatever. You have a million rooms in this house, we can just use one of them."

I grabbed the glass from Andrei when he walked over with my drink. I just wanted something to do with my hands, to hide my awkwardness with the simple motion of putting a cup to my lips. I took a sip. Sweet. Tart. The vodka scorched my throat.

Drinking wasn't an entirely new experience. Anita's older sister bought us all coolers once, when we were fifteen—a bribe to keep our mouths shut about the thirty-five-year-old man she was seeing. Even my mother had celebrated my acceptances with two glasses of Prosecco. But this felt different. Justin watched me, his eyes fixed on my expression, and I took a larger gulp, forbidding myself to cough.

Ryan Collingwood turned to me from the sofa, holding out his freshly rolled joint. "Toke?"

I waved my free hand. "I'm good."

"Really?" He kept his arm outstretched. "Aren't you, like, Jamaican or something?"

"Ryan!" Hannah shoved him, laughing incredulously. "Don't be such a racist."

"What are you talking about? How was that racist?"

She shook her head. "Kara's Canadian anyway."

I drank more to keep from having to talk. By the time Nora and Sebastian showed up, I was halfway through my third glass. The rest of the afternoon swirled by me in a warm haze: Justin and Nora chasing each other up the stairs. Hannah and Ryan passing the joint back and forth. Andrei staring at me curiously, like I had the secrets to the universe, like if he asked the right questions I would have no choice but to share them with him.

"How long does it take you to get your hair like that?" he asked. "So wait, what's a weave, then?"

When I finally decided to leave, it took me a minute to remember how to balance myself. Walking wasn't difficult but my body felt light, weightless; I was watching myself move instead of actually causing the movements. It was lucky my mother had moved us downtown, that I didn't have to take a bus and then a train all the way up to Eglinton West or Wilson and Bathurst, that this home was only about twenty minutes away.

She was in the kitchen when I stumbled through the front door. The stink of macaroni and cheese polluted the air and made my stomach churn.

"Kara?" Her voice was sharp. It rattled in my head. "What are you doing home?"

I had an answer for this. I'd prepared one just in case I ran into her or anyone who knew her. I'd prepared another one for if I ran into Nana or any of the church ladies she shared a pew with, even though they were never downtown. And I'd prepared one in case I ran into a teacher or a secretary on the sidewalk, a janitor on a lunch break.

My mother kept pushing. "Kara, answer me when I talk to you. What are you doing home?"

I remember the sound of boiling water, the blurry sight of my mother turning away from the stove. The television was on and our one window was open. I remember opening my mouth to speak, to gift her one of my excuses, and then I remember bending over, hands on my knees, and hurling on the spot.

3.

The problem was, I only apologized for the vomit.

It was the next morning. Throughout the night I'd gulped down three glasses of water and put a dent in my hunger with two slices of unbuttered toast, throwing up only one more time. My mother hadn't talked to me the entire time but now she clattered around in the kitchen, banging down mugs and pots and slamming cupboard doors shut, muttering loudly as if I weren't a few feet away from her.

"Likkle girl think she grown because she turned eighteen. Is she crazy? Hmph. She must'a not know who I am."

I'd never heard my mother speak in an accent before. An image of Nana unfurled in my mind, of when she was angry and when that anger pushed her to move, pushed her to pace the hall and pound her fists, pushed her to yell, to claim the entire house with her voice, but kept her from speaking to the cause of her rage, kept her from admitting that another person had triggered such a response. It was a rage my mother inherited, and hearing the accent and seeing my mother ease into that same kind of fury was what got me to speak more than anything else. I sat myself up on the sofa bed before taking a breath.

"I'm sorry."

My mother took out a thin box of peppermint tea before saying anything. "I don't care if you don't like tea; this will settle your stomach so you're drinking every last drop of it."

"Okay," I said.

She was about to reach for the small black pot she used for boiling water or eggs but stopped, her hand suspended above the handle. "'Okay?'" Her voice was a warning.

"Thanks?"

"'Yes, Mom.'"

I was supposed to parrot it back to her, correct my mistake. The response had always been standard. Ingrained from childhood. But all I wanted to do was lie back down and cradle my head or hold my stomach, keep myself from falling apart.

"Well?"

All I could bring myself to do was repeat myself. "I'm sorry."

"What are you sorry for, Kara?"

"For throwing up in the house."

My mother turned around and leaned against the counter. Her lips were drawn into a tight line, their fullness obscured by anger. She folded her arms across her small chest.

"Is that it?"

I didn't say anything.

"Speak, girl," she said.

I knew what the right answer was. I knew what she wanted me to say and how she wanted me to say it—but I wasn't able to say anything else, to show her that I knew what she expected of me. When I didn't break my silence, my mother slammed her palm onto the countertop, the rings on her middle and index fingers banging against the linoleum. After a few seconds, she slammed her palm again, and I was stricken with the image of her hand across my face. It'd been years since she'd hit me but she knew how to conjure up those memories in my head; she knew how to inflate her presence, make herself bigger with the noise she created, the shouts she bellowed.

"You think I don't know about rebelling?" she said. "About the 'It's my life' bullshit? You think I haven't been there? Do not try it with me, likkle gyal, you are not one of those kids at that damn school."

The ranting didn't stop when she turned back around to prepare the tea. It reached that pitch it got to sometimes, when the words were garbled and incoherent because the anger had taken over and all she could do was yell. It was almost otherworldly—I used to wonder if my mother was actually *here* when she started screeching. Now, I put my hands to my head, pressing my fingertips to my temples, inwardly screaming at her to just shut up.

"What was she thinking? Tell me, what was she thinking?"

I stared at her back, at the opportunity it gave me.

"Everyone said I was too young for this. Can you believe it? She ah come home drunk like a damn *skunk!*"

I stood up and briefly touched the back pocket of my jeans, more out of instinct than intention, a habit to see if my phone was there. I didn't care about the apartment keys. My running shoes were on the floor by the sofa bed where I'd kicked them off in my sleep the night before. I didn't bother putting them on properly and my heels flattened the notches. My mother's voice swelled, her screaming rising even higher, and I left the apartment, taking nothing else with me.

4.

The next stop is Queen. Queen station.

I wished for a panic attack. Hyperventilation. Tears. Anything to show the weight of what I'd done. But my body didn't allow me any messy relief; I sat on the train dry-eyed and numbed.

Every time the train pulled into a station I wondered if this was where I should get off, if I should leave the subway and walk the streets, wander a city I lived in but never explored. It seemed safer to stay cocooned in the invisibility that came with being underground, that came with being unreachable. But when the train reached Union Station, I made up my mind to get off, maybe visit the Hockey Hall of Fame and just ignore the unrelenting phone calls of my mother instead of hiding from them. The doors slid open with a *ding* and I envisioned myself walking through them but then stiffened with an abrupt dread.

Aishani Bhakta ran into the train car before the doors slid shut, her long plait swinging at her back. She was wearing a McDonald's baseball cap and a black-and-grey uniform, and shouldering one of those Puma cinch bags I'd always wanted. The train kept moving, continuing its course north, and I looked back out the window even though I knew she'd seen me.

"Now I know you're not about to pretend like you don't know me," she said.

I turned my head to look at her. She stood with her hands on her hips and one of her eyebrows quirked. Her eyes were tired.

"Why not?" I said. "You do it to me all the time."

Aishani sat down in the seat across from me, taking off her cap and loosening her black hair from the plait. "Anita said that moving downtown made you stush."

"Anita says a lot of things."

"You nuh lie. I heard you're doing big t'ings, still though," said Aishani. Even after all of these years, her attempt at a Trini accent hadn't gotten any better.

"Rochelle can't keep your name out of her mouth," she explained.

I shrugged but didn't answer. The question was a test anyway, a way to determine if Anita was right or wrong about how much I'd changed.

I glanced at her silver nameplate. "So you're working down here now? At Union Station?"

"Kind of like a promotion," she said. "I'm up for manager in a couple of months."

"That's cool."

She kissed her teeth. "Why are you so rude for?"

"I was being serious, Shani."

"Oh." She leaned against the chair and tilted her head back so that it rested against the window behind her. She sighed heavily. "I can never tell anymore."

"Is that what you're going to do, then?" I asked. "When school's done."

Aishani furrowed her eyebrows and I grinned. "Rochelle talks *everyone's* business," I said.

"That girl is going to get a box one day." She shook her head. "I don't really know what I want to do after school's done," she said.

"You have some time left, so I guess that's okay."

"Not according to my parents," she said. "I'd be the first in my family to go to university, you know."

"Yeah," I said. "That's pretty big."

She stretched out her legs and stared at the tips of her black running shoes, looking like she wanted to dive into the floor.

"Can we not talk about this?" she asked.

"Yeah, sure."

Neither of us said anything after that and when the train left St. George station Aishani closed her eyes. I turned back to the window, looking out to the black tunnels of the subway, my eyes focused on nothing in particular. The hardness of my cellphone pressed against my jeans and dimpled my thigh. I shifted to get more comfortable.

Arriving at Eglinton West. Eglinton West station.

We were above ground now, the tunnels quickly giving way to views of yellow-green grass and speeding cars on the highway. Aishani lurched awake and was on her feet before I realized what was happening. She grabbed onto a pole and spun around to the other side of it, like we used to do when we were kids.

"Coming?"

The train rolled to a stop.

"Maybe later," I said.

The doors opened and Aishani stepped onto the platform. "My number hasn't changed," she said.

"Right."

Step away from the doors; the doors are now closing.

Aishani was already halfway up the stairs when the train started up again, clattering toward Glencairn station. My phone vibrated with notifications. Twenty-five missed calls, all from my mother. Her stalkerish tenacity wasn't surprising, but it filled me with resentment. When my call display lit up with the word MOM for her twenty-sixth call, I pressed my forehead against the glass of the window, squeezing the phone with my right hand. When she called me for the twenty-ninth time, I picked up.

"Where the hell are you? Do you know how close I was to calling the police? The police, Kara? I should kill you." Her heavy breathing made my throat tighten and my thumb itched to press the End button.

"You can't do this. You cannot afford to act out like this. When you get back here, I want you to write me a report telling me exactly how you got the alcohol, where you were when you weren't at school, and a list of names of the kids you were with. Are you listening to me? You may go to their school but you cannot afford to act like them. You have to be better than this, Kara." There was a tremor in her voice, a quiver I rarely heard. It wasn't anger and it wasn't sadness. It was something different, something she never meant for me to notice. Fear.

"Are you listening to me?"

"I'm listening," I said.

"Get your ass back home."

5.

I hung up after she did. We stopped at Lawrence West station. Across from me, on the other side of the platform, a southbound train rested on the tracks, its doors open. A kid in a white shirt pulled on his mother's dress.

"Why isn't the train moving? We've been here forever!"

I could make it. If I got up now and sprinted across the platform to the other side, I could get onto the train and head back downtown and home. I kept my head turned to the window and stared at those open doors, at the commuters crammed into the car, frustrated and impatient. I stared at them as my train's doors closed, as we started moving up the track. I stared at where the open doors would be even as we pulled out of Lawrence West and chugged toward the next station.

FRYING PLANTAIN

1.

When Nana calls our apartment for the fifth time in the same week I am sent over to her house. The voicemail she leaves, vague mutterings about a dream she had of me, makes my mother's eye jump and she dispatches me to the bungalow for the full story; dreams aren't something to be messed around with. If a family member has one of another member, it's their duty to report it—not to do so would be spiteful. But when I get off the train and push past the turnstiles to the subway's exit, I don't make it to Nana's front door. I don't even make it to her block. The thought of listening to Nana's ramblings on the prophetic powers of vivid dreams makes me stay on Eglinton Avenue West. I get swept up in the alien familiarity of a neighbourhood I once lived in but haven't been back to in two years, not since I was seventeen.

Nothing about it has changed.

It's still the type of neighbourhood that never rests, never stays quiet. The cars that drive through take ownership of the air, their stereos blasting ragga ragga or soca, the bass so loud I can feel it in the sidewalk beneath my feet. I look directly ahead of me and move quickly past the storefronts where boys, as usual, hold court or roll dice, only ever standing up straight and curbing their catcalls when mothers and church women pass by.

I go into one of the jerk chicken shops that plays roots reggae for the old-timers and I eat my chicken and rice at the window, watching the pedestrians amble past, watching the men slapping down dominoes. The men sit on crates, laughing loudly at the crass jokes they tell each other. I wonder if Rochelle will be one of the people I see pass by the store. It's been ages since I've spoken to any of my childhood friends, but Rochelle is the one who held on the longest. She and I congratulated each other on our university acceptances, on the new lives we'd start as undergrads, and then forgot to share those lives with each other. I'm not even sure if she still lives on Hopewell Avenue or if she moved out to be closer to campus, but the possibility of seeing her makes me both nervous and excited.

When my mother asks me what happened I tell her Nana didn't answer the door when I knocked, a story I stick to even after she points out that Nana stays home more now that she's retired, even after Nana calls us and says she never heard me stop by. The sixth time Nana leaves a message, a week later, my mother tells me to try her house again.

2.

Sundays, when I was in primary school, I was sent to Nana's so she could take me to church. My mother would struggle to get me into a velvet gown or a satin dress and as she sat me on the couch to force me into a pair of pantyhose she'd say, "I don't want you to cause any trouble today, you hear me?"

"Yes, Mom."

"I mean it, Kara. If Nana calls me and tells me you were rude, I will slap you when you get home. You understand?"

I nodded.

"Okay, good. Now give me a kiss."

Nana lived one street over from us on Whitmore Avenue — we were still on Belgravia then — and we always met her on her veranda at seven thirty. After my mother handed me over, only nodding at my grandmother both in hello and farewell, she'd go back home to bed. She used to tell me that Sundays were the only days she could rest fully; that tutoring, office work, and school ate up her weekdays with no remorse, in the evenings I was no better, greedy for her attention, demanding of her energy. She needed Sundays to restore her soul, which was one more reason why I should behave with Nana.

Once Nana and I were on the train northbound to her congregation, the reprimands would start spilling out. "Stop swingin' yuh legs"; "Stop itchin' yuh stockin'"; "Stop singin' that song fi today is Sunday and we only sing gospel on the Lord's Day." I never said anything right away; it was at church that I began to act up, that I complained about how hot it was, ran around with the boys, touched the feathers and bows on every wide-brimmed hat in front of me. Whenever Nana caught me she'd say, "Nuh act like a likkle pickney, God want yuh fi be a good likkle gyal, nuh play rough with the boys them." I'd grumble and then she'd take me over to her friends, a different group of women each time, and I'd stand behind her and stare at the boys playing tag.

"Kara. *Kara*. Tell Sister Ida what yuh want fi be."

"A pediatrician."

"Hear that?" she'd say. "My granddaughter gwine fi be a *pediatrician*. Teachers them think she bright yuh know." She'd look at me to smile sweetly, and I'd pout and tug on her dress to signal I was ready to leave.

The afternoons were the only part of Sundays I liked. When church was over we'd head back to Eglinton West and Marlee, where she'd take me to Randy's Takeout for a beef patty and coco bread. Once we were at her house she didn't talk to me much, which suited me fine. She'd change out of her church suit and into her housedress and after heating up lunch for me, she'd start to prepare dinner and clean, her incessant vacuuming overpowering any other sound in the house.

My mother would pick me up in the early evening, and by that time I'd have already eaten, usually curry chicken and rice, or a bowl of dumpling stew (I never ate the ackee and saltfish that came with it). Nana would send me out the door with old margarine containers filled with leftovers; my mother never asked to come in for dinner and Nana never invited her to. Soon, leaving the bungalow took over as the only part of Sunday I liked, and it wasn't too long before I begged my mother not to send me over anymore.

3.

Nana's street is just off Eglinton West and Marlee, a little residential pocket hidden behind the stores and surrounded by maples. Everything about her bungalow is the same as it's always been—the painted pale blue stoop, the *Jesus Watches* doormat, the black tarmac driveway, oil-slicked from my grandfather's car. The only thing that's different is the lawn. When I was younger, campaign signs from each political party littered the green and Nana wouldn't get rid of them even after elections were over. I never minded it much, mostly laughed at the Conservative blue, Liberal red, and NDP orange intermingling on a lump of grass, but the signs drove my mother crazy. Every time we left the house, she'd seem to think they would disappear in our absence; when we'd come back to find them still pitched into the grass she would get infuriated all over again.

"There's just no need for this many signs," she would say, storming into the kitchen, gesturing at Nana's back.

"I don't want fi hear it, Eloise."

"They're taking advantage of you! Do you even know what half of these parties are?"

"Eh-eh, I am not schupid!"

Sometimes my mother responded, sometimes she'd walk away.

I only have to knock once before Nana opens the

door, and when she does, she stares at me with those appraising eyes I remember so well. She hasn't changed much. A woman dedicated to maintaining a youthful appearance, she's been able to keep her face quite smooth despite reaching her mid-sixties. She's a stout woman, but shapely enough for anyone to see that she'd been curvy once. Her facial expression is exactly how I remember it, too: repulsed and vaguely surprised, like she's just bitten into a bitter lime and is starting to feel the shock of it fill up her mouth.

"Hi, Nana."

"I canna believe it. Yuh came."

"You called."

"When I called yuh last week yuh nuh come visit me."

"I already told you what happened with that."

"Mm-hmm." She leans against the doorway and pushes out her mouth, her arms crossed and her eyes slowly passing over my body. Her gaze starts at the top of my head and makes its way down to my feet, and I feel relieved by my decision to dress up for the visit, to wear a peasant skirt that reaches my ankles instead of my usual pedal-pushers.

"Yuh need some Vaseline on yuh foot there, suh," she says, finally. "It dry like ash." She moves from the doorway, and I fantasize about walking away without a word, heading back to the main street, ignoring her phone calls, my mother's expectant gazes, for the rest of my life.

But I follow Nana into the house, careful to move my sandals to the side after I take them off on the welcome mat in the foyer. The crystal bowl full of red-and-white peppermint candies is still on the curved accent table, there for the neighbourhood kids who sometimes carry her grocery bags and regale her with hard-to-get gossip. I look to the left through the archway. The living room, carpeted in Oriental designs, is exactly how I remember it—filled with furniture all washed in tones of deep red. The mahogany china cabinet filled with Royal Henry tea sets still stands in a corner with a copy of the Royal Standard of Jamaica pinned above it, a print of the Royal Wedding next to the flag. Two Louis armchairs sit at either end of the camelback sofa that, ever since my childhood, has been enveloped in plastic covering, a "Keep Foot Off" note right above it. Directly across from the couch is the dining table, dividing the kitchen from the living room. As always, even though the television is on, she also has the radio tuned to a station dedicated to gospel and scripture. The same gold anniversary clock I once threw on the floor sits next to the stereo, mint and encased in a glass dome like it was never broken.

"If yuh want fi sit on the chesterfield then sit," says
Nana as she closes the door and walks straight down
the foyer and into the kitchen. "Yuh don't haffi stand
there all day."

"I'm good. Thanks."

"Well, if yuh change yuh mind."

"Then I'll sit."

She nods her head and then turns on the sink's faucet. There are only a couple of dirty dishes but she rubs
her hands together like she's about to work through a
big load. I turn to the door that leads to the basement.
She rents it out now, but when I was three or four it was
where my father and I spent our evenings before he left
my mother and me to live in it alone. My father and I
would watch TV at low volume or play-fight quietly
until my mother came in from night school. It was only
then that he felt comfortable venturing up to the dining
room to eat dinner while my mother decompressed
downstairs and Nana showered for bed. Once, running
up the stairs, I tripped, scraping my chin against the
floor. Nana had been watching from the bathroom, her
eyebrows raised, and when my mother realized I'd be
okay, she whispered, "Don't cry. Suck it up." That's how
she always instructed me in front of Nana. In whispers.

Nana calls out from the kitchen. "Yuh hungry? I
have plantain here."

"That's fine. I ate before I came."

"Yuh tellin' mi yuh belly so full yuh canna even have a likkle snack?"

The clock on the kitchen wall says it's four. In an hour and a half the music store around the corner will be closed and I've been looking forward to going, to thumbing through the rocksteady records that the stores by my building don't stock. I don't want to stay here long.

"Nana, I am not that hungry."

She barrels toward me and pinches my upper arm, making me jerk away from her. "Yuh skinny, *mawga,* like a stray cat. I tell yuh, say, one windy day yuh gwine fi walk on the street there suh and the breeze gwine fi pick yuh up and go! Come now, I start fi cook."

I could insist on leaving, but instead I only groan as she turns off the faucet and wipes her hands on a tea towel, moving toward the cupboard for her skillet. I lean against the basement door and dig my fingernails beneath my braids, scratching my scalp so I can have something to do with my hands.

Nana's frown relaxes when she puts her knife to the plantain, and even though I don't want to be, I'm impressed by the way she slices off the skin. The way she peels plantain has always impressed me. The blade just slides through like nothing; there's no sign of effort or struggle. I don't see the blade tug at the toughness of the skin like when I do it. This looks easy; this looks like the plantain is undressing itself. A kind of content mindlessness passes over Nana's face, making me feel a gentle uncertainty toward her that makes me uncomfortable. The peels drop onto the counter and she starts shaving the plantain into long slices. I want to tell her to just make circles, that that's how I like it, but I just grunt instead, reminding myself not to get too involved in the process, that I'm not staying long. The pieces fall into the frying pan with every slice of the knife, sizzling as they land.

"I know yuh nuh eat like this no more," she says, pushing around the plantain with a fork.

"I do sometimes."

Nana laughs harshly. "When? Yuh mother nuh teach you how fi cook, she nuh learn how fi cook from me. I nuh have no education but I know how fi cook."

"No one said anything about edu—" I sigh. "Yes, Nana."

"I could have teach yuh, yuh know, I could teach yuh still, but yuh never stop by."

"I'm never really in this part of the city anymore."

She turns down the stove and moves her dutchie pot from the front burner to the back, replacing it with a second frying pan for the eggs.

"Scramble or fry? Oh I know yuh like yuh eggs them fry, nuh true?"

"Nana—yes."

She cracks the shell over the side of the pan and the scent is immediate. The clock says only seven minutes have passed.

"Kara, get me the cinnamon from the pantry."

Her voice is so gruff I almost tell her to get it herself—but her voice is always hard. I step into the kitchen and open the pantry doors above the sink. It's strange delving deeper into this house; moving from the foyer into the kitchen feels like abandoning my safety line and my escape, and I try my best to appear calm, to not betray the thudding in my chest. I give Nana the cinnamon and she sprinkles it on the plantain.

"No brown sugar?"

"A'right, that too," she says, with what seems to be a hint of a grin pulling at the corner of her lips. "Get it. I'm just gwine fi put a stip."

Even as a child, I couldn't understand how she could cook without using measurements and still make a meal that didn't turn out disastrously; it's a trick I've never learned. She shakes a pinch of brown sugar over the frying fruit and then turns the pieces over.

"How's the neighbourhood?" I ask. "It seems good."

"It's a'right. I haffi praise Jesus yuh make it here safe."

"It seems as safe now as it was when we lived here."

"I did not say that it nuh safe. I just know that the boys them need discipline in their lives," she says, flipping over the egg.

4.

Our second stint at Nana's house only lasted five months, but even after we left her bungalow, left the neighbourhood, I'd find myself walking up and down Eglinton West as much as I could, starting from Marlee and sometimes going as far as Keele. There were no jerk chicken shops or hairdressers that could braid or relax or twist hair into sisterlocks in the areas my mother moved us to. The schools I attended, those neighbourhoods just had colonies of fast-food chains and music stores that blasted American Top 40 from their speakers. Even the Shoppers Drug Marts were a letdown. Stores with row upon row of mousses and volumizers; white, thin-lipped faces on the bottles. The one time I asked for texture softener, the cashier told me to find a store farther west.

"That's what the storefinder says," he said.

Each time I'd visited this neighbourhood, either to spend my Saturday in the salon or spend it catching up with the friends I'd had to leave, I never once considered walking past the 7-Eleven and down the pathway to visit Nana. I never even thought I would see her on the main street; she did all of her grocery shopping after church. Back then, weekdays and Saturdays she worked her two jobs in the suburbs and came home at midnight, sometimes half past.

The day I saw her, it was a summer afternoon, the hottest day in July, and I'd worn a turquoise sundress that fell to my ankles but had a V-neck neckline. When I walked by the boys who hung out in front of the Graphic Tees store, one of them stopped me to ask my name, his friends encouraging him loudly, yelling, "C'mon, he's a nice guy! Give him your number, girl!"

I don't remember seeing her walk up to us but there she was next to me, her voice louder and harsher than all of them.

"Kara!"

"Nana?"

"How yuh walkin' around suh? With yuh titties a-door!"

"*Nana!*"

Some of the older boys clapped their hands over their mouths to keep from laughing, but a few of the younger ones bolted, either hopped on their bikes or just flat-out ran, probably afraid they'd see Nana in church with their mothers or grandmothers or aunts.

"Yuh best fi come with me now," she said, using her

body to guide me away from the store. "Acting fresh with the boys them, yuh too slack!"

"I wasn't—"

"Hush up and come! Lord have mercy."

"I wasn't doing anything! They just—"

"I will not help yuh raise no pickney, yuh know."

"Nana—"

"Hush up!"

Only when we were in her house did she allow me to slip in a word or two. She sat me at the dining table and listened to my explanation while wiping down the kitchen counter with a tea towel. When I finished, she watched me for a moment.

"A'right," she said. "A'right."

She opened the fridge and took out a fresh black cake. She'd made it strong. The moment she took off the plastic wrap, I could smell the rum even though I was sitting a few feet away. She cut me a slice and gave me some carrot juice.

"Yuh need fi be careful," she said when I started to eat. "When the boys them come up to yuh, tell them yuh waitin' for yuh father or yuh boyfriend. Yuh hear me?"

"Yes, Nana."

"Good."

I'd called my mother to tell her what happened—

better she heard it from me than from Nana or some other passerby — and thirty minutes later, she was honking the horn by the driveway, luring me outside. But Nana was out the door before I was.

"How can yuh let her walk around with clothes like this?"

My mother threw her head back against her seat and sighed. "Do you know how hot it is outside? She's dressed fine."

"Yuh should've seen the way them boys was lookin' at her, Eloise."

"Was she doing anything with them?"

"I was there fi stop anything from happenin'."

"So you're telling me if you weren't there then Kara would've done something?"

"I did not say—"

"So then stop interfering with my child, Verna. Kara's a sensible girl. She knows how to handle herself."

"Sensible? How yuh gwine fi talk about being 'sensible'? I remember yuh was a sensible girl too and look what happened, pregnant at seventeen!"

I saw it before Nana did, the shift in my mother's eyes, the tightening of her hands on the steering wheel. Before I could stop it from happening, she was out of the car, and the two were screaming at each other, leaning into each other's faces, oblivious to the ogling eyes peering out from semi-drawn curtains and closed blinds. I braced myself, watching every gesture and making sure they didn't graduate to a slap or a push or a hair-pull.

"You were Kara's age when yuh start fi stay out all hours of the night!"

"With a mother like you, how the hell could I not? All that goddamn yelling and cleaning I couldn't go anywhere—"

"At least I clean my place! Yuh take no pride in yuh house, yuh nuh clean, yuh nuh cook, yuh nuh go fi church, yuh canna raise a daughter proper!"

"I swear to God if you bring up Kara one more time—"

"What yuh gwine fi do, hmm? You think yuh a bad woman? Test me!"

When the neighbours became bolder with their prying and stood out on their porches for a better view of the fight, Nana returned to her house and my mother and I got into the car and drove away. My mother turned down the next side street and parked beneath the shade of a large oak tree and screamed until I was sure she'd shredded her throat. She pounded the steering wheel, cursing, and I sat still with my face toward the windshield and my eyes closed.

She turned the ignition back on. "I don't want you coming up here anymore," she said.

5.

The plantain and eggs are done now, and Nana is putting two pieces of bread in the toaster. I am standing by the fridge, a few inches away from the foyer, and wonder when she's going to *tsk* me for blocking the entryway even though I doubt anyone will be strolling in.

The house smells sweet and crisp, and my eyes fix themselves on the plate of food on the counter, Nana's body bustling around it, putting the pans in the sink to soak. The pop of the toaster startles me into checking the time again. Half an hour has passed since the last time I checked.

"Yuh want something fi drink?"

"I'll just grab something." I open the fridge and Nana heads over to me. "I nuh want yuh fi trouble my fridge," she says. "I put everything in its place proper. Gwaan and sit down, I will bring it to yuh."

White linen covers the oval dining table as a first layer and then Nana has draped the linen over in a plastic sheet. Cloth placemats and lace doilies are in two separate piles around the floral centrepiece. Beneath all the layers the table is a deep, dark wood. I remember her smile when she made her last layaway payment for it one day after church. The store owner liked Nana so much he had his son deliver it to the house even though it was a Sunday, and she paid him to discard the birch wood table she was replacing.

I take my seat and before I even settle in, Nana puts down my plate and a tall glass of Kola Champagne on a lace doily, then sits down next to me. It's always a little strange when she sits, when she stops moving for just a moment and disregards the fact that things have to get done. It's the same thing with my mother. Except that her energy is quiet, potent but below the surface, so when she's no longer moving, there's a slight shift in the atmosphere. Nana's loud. Robust. When she's still, everything around her seems to slow down.

I pick up my fork and she watches me put the plantain in my mouth—she's outwardly calm but it feels like she's holding her breath. When I nod my head at the sweetness seeping into my tongue, she leans back in her chair.

"Nuh too dry?"

"No," I say. "It's great."

She lets me eat without talking for a while, smoothing her hands over the plastic. "So how is school?"

"It's good. Hard. Lots of work. I can't wait to graduate."

"Mm. Yes, I know it's hard work since yuh gwine fi study fi be a pediatrician inna university."

I chew slowly. "I was nine when I said that. I'm nineteen now. Things change."

"So what yuh study inna university?"

"Cinema Studies."

"'Cinema Studies'?" She twists her mouth as she repeats those words back to me, like she's trying to taste each letter, extract some significance. I can't help but picture her enduring the work she used to do, how for years, she'd wake up in the wee hours of the morning to clean bedpans and turn sheets, gritting her teeth when those she looked after forgot we were in the millennium and called her nigger girl and black bitch. I clear my throat loudly.

"Tell me about the dream, Nana."

"Yuh nuh care about dream. You are a *Canadian* girl," she says, putting on an accent and laughing to herself.

"I still know to come when called about a dream."

She stares at me intently and then begins to speak slowly, her voice clear with purpose. "I dream about hands, hands held up to some woman's mouth. And when she take way them hands, all her teeth just crumbled away, yuh understand? I take few, few steps back to see who the woman was. The woman's face ah look like Eloise."

I take a sip of the soda and try to look ponderous. Losing dream teeth, I know, is a bad sign. "Mom will probably think a duppy is following her," I say.

"Eh-eh, nuh make light of such things, Kara. Duppy them evil spirit, drive yuh crazy, make yuh mad, tear up yuh whole life."

"You told me this when you told me about the duppy tree when I was small."

"Never too old for lessons. Duppies have been around long before yuh were born, long before any of us."

"That's what Mom says," I say.

Nana lets air out of her mouth like a whistle. "Yuh mother is right about some things."

6.

I was going into my first year of high school when my mother told me we would be living with Nana. It was a decision I'd known about before she told me, a favour I'd overheard her ask my grandmother during Christmas dinner. But it wasn't until May, until a week before we had to make the move, that she felt like cluing me in.

I got home from school, and she told me we were going out. Any restaurant I wanted. I knew then that she was warming up for upsetting me. She waited until

I took a bite out of my fifteen-dollar hamburger and then said it.

"We'll be living with Nana for a while."

I drank all of the Coke in my glass in an attempt to plan my reaction but all I could think to say was, "Why?"

"Because we need to."

"But *why*?"

"Because I said so." She took a sip of the martini she'd ordered. "Now stop talking and eat."

It took us three sleepless nights to move all of our things out of the apartment on Belgravia. We shoved our furniture into Nana's garage and brought our clothes into the house. I even got to bring the little TV my mother had bought me for Christmas when I was eight.

It was fine at first, almost perfect. Nana seemed glad to have someone to cook for every day since my grandfather was ghosting again, only dropping by every once in a while for a meal and late-night company. Plantain and eggs for breakfast. Curry goat and rice and peas for dinner. She even packed my lunches: real ham and turkey sandwiches on baguettes from the bakery just by the men's clothing boutique.

It was a month into our move that things started to turn. The changes were gradual but they weren't subtle. Nights Nana would come home and grumble about our presence, how we upset her routine, the way she set up the kitchen. My mother and I spent more and more time in our bedroom, only leaving it to use the bathroom and take showers. Sometimes we'd stay out past midnight, driving to the suburbs, looking at the square houses with their square lawns and sprinkler systems, hoping Nana would have wiped herself out and gone to bed by the time we got back to the house.

The fights began in September, when school started up again. One morning I was too tired to eat breakfast and I fell asleep at the table. The night before, Nana had come home to find a few grains of rice on the kitchen counter and she just lost it: she clattered pots and pans, banged on the walls, vacuumed right by our bedroom door, bellowed insults disguised as hymns.

"I invite them inna my house and I get rice inna my kitchen! All of them MESSY! All of them STINK! Canna even pick up after themselves! Lord have mercy! What did I do fi deserve this?"

By the time she'd fallen silent, there was an hour left until I had to wake up for school and my mother for work. At the table, when I could hardly lift up my head, my mother slammed the cereal box down and wrenched open Nana's door.

"My daughter can't stay awake long enough to eat her breakfast."

"Yuh canna just come inna my room—"

"My daughter can't—"

"Well yuh canna just leave messes inna mi house! Yuh a nasty woman!"

"And you're crazy! I mean it, you're sick!"

My mother didn't hide anymore after that. Every time Nana started to complain she matched her, insult for insult. Yell for yell. Slammed-down pan for slammed-down pan. I learned to sleep lightly, enough to feel rested and enough to hear what was going on in the living room to make sure that, for all their talk, nothing violent actually happened.

One night my mother and I had been out driving until three in the morning only to find the door chained when we got back.

"Maybe she thought we wouldn't be coming back tonight?"

She didn't respond. She didn't even look at me. She jabbed her finger into the doorbell, making one long continuous ring, until the lights came on and we saw Nana moving toward us through the small space of the semi-open door.

"Get off mi porch," she said. "I don't want yuh here. I canna take it no more! Yuh nuh follow my rules! Yuh bedroom messy! Mi can smell the Macdonal' yuh eat inna yuh room!"

"Why are you in our bedroom?"

"This is my house! I go where I want fi go!"

"It's three in the morning, where are we supposed to go?"

"I nuh care!" Nana tried to close the door all the way but my mother pushed against it to keep it open and then rammed through it with her shoulder, breaking off the copper chain. I didn't dare follow her inside the house or try to stop her from hurtling the dishes and tea sets onto the floor, from tearing down the paintings on the walls, from tracking dirt onto the carpets, smudging it in with the heel of her pumps.

I stood on the stoop and watched, holding back tears, knowing she'd scream at me later if she caught me crying. We left only when Nana threatened to call the police. I didn't speak for the rest of the night; my mother's rage ran deep and possessed her for long periods of time, and I knew from experience that silence was the best way to maintain peace.

The next day was Saturday, so I went back to Nana's early in the morning to beg her to put us up for one more week.

"Just until we get an apartment," I said.

She stopped scrubbing the carpet and turned to look

at me, slowly getting off her hands and knees. "After she come inna mi house and mash up everything?"

"Just one week."

"Kara, I said no!"

"We slept in our car last night. Can you please just do this for me?"

She finally picked up a bottle of dish detergent and then turned around and looked at me. "Yuh have one week. One week and yuh go."

"Thank you."

7.

It's late in the afternoon. A little after five thirty. Nana has begun seasoning a chicken for tomorrow, Sunday, night. Right now she's sweeping in the kitchen even though there's nothing on the floor to sweep. Details like that don't matter to her, though. Something always needs cleaning. Something always needs polishing. It made me tense as a child—watching her create work for herself, when she saw it as keeping the Devil at bay.

"I should get going," I say.

"Yuh haffi go already?"

"It's getting late."

She stops sweeping, leans the broom against the counter, and walks up to me. "Have some bun and cheese before yuh leave."

"No, it's okay," I say, standing up and heading toward the foyer. "I don't really feel for it."

"Well how about some ice cream? I know yuh always want chocolate ice cream and I have some in the freezer somewhere."

"I'm actually pretty full."

"Yes, I know how yuh get full easy. Let mi make some mint tea. It will help sekkle yuh stomach."

"I don't like tea."

"I know that but—"

"Nana!" I say. "I just want to go home, okay?"

There's a pause and for a second I think she might yell, slap me even and run the risk of dealing with my mother, but she just clears her throat and walks back into the kitchen.

"Yes, yuh have a long way back home."

She turns to the dishwasher and opens its door, pulling out the racks; they're filled with plastic bags and empty yogurt cups. I don't think she's ever used it to wash dishes. She fills a couple of the yogurt cups with the rest of the plantain and some leftover oxtail and rice from the fridge, putting everything in a yellow No Frills bag.

"Take this home and share it with yuh mother."

"Okay," I say quietly, taking the bag from her. "I will."

"A'right, then."

She stands on the threshold between the kitchen and the foyer and watches as I put on my sandals. My eyes land on a painting, a colourful print of a Jamaican marketplace by the coast, slightly, almost barely, torn; a near-casualty of that night.

"Make sure yuh share that, nuh," says Nana.

I nod my head and tighten my grip on the No Frills bag, feeling the weight of the margarine containers and yogurt cups, remembering the weight of all of the leftovers she'd given me throughout the years. I smile slightly and turn toward the door. "Thank you for the food, Nana."

ACKNOWLEDGEMENTS

There were many times in the years it took to write this collection that I thought it would never get published, that I had accumulated a massive amount of student debt in the pursuit of a goal I would never achieve, that I was a fraud to call myself a "writer." I would like to thank all of the people who were instrumental in making my first book a reality (buckle in, it's a long list).

Thank you to House of Anansi for giving this first-timer such an incredible publishing experience, for being approachable and accessible and sensitive to my artistic choices. In relation, I would like to express my gratitude to Amelia Spedaliere, who had such passionate faith in my manuscript and who encouraged me to take my time to develop it into the collection it is now before resubmitting it for consideration.

I would like to thank my agent, Amy Tompkins, for taking a chance on an unknown writer with a short story collection (not a novel!), and for being my champion.

Thank you to my editor, Melanie Little, for taking the time to really understand my work, for being receptive but not complacent, for giving me thoughtful and painstaking comments.

In my experience, having supportive, talented, and challenging teachers and instructors is integral to artistic growth, so I would like to take this opportunity to acknowledge the ones who contributed to mine.

Thank you, Ibi Kaslik, my first mentor, for encouraging me to go back to my collection when I had nearly given up on it, for being the first one to say, "I want to see this in a bookstore." To George Elliott Clarke, an overwhelmingly generous adviser, thank you for providing instruction that still stays with me whenever I write, and thank you for never hesitating to help me advance, whether it's through a reference letter or advice.

I would like to thank the instructors I had while attending Columbia University. Thank you to Alana Newhouse, whose patience and ability to ask the right questions encouraged me to be more vulnerable on the page; to Paul Beatty, whose critical eye and willingness to discuss creative fears and intentions helped me find my voice; and to Victor Lavalle, who provided blunt and uncompromising discussions about my work that led me to overcome barriers I never knew I had.

I would also like to thank Janice Galloway and Greg Hollingshead. Without their guidance, this collection would have no message.

Of course, thank you to the Ontario Arts Council and the Toronto Arts Council for providing funding that allowed me the necessary time to edit my work.

I would be remiss not to thank my employers at Diaspora Dialogues and Avana Capital, Helen Walsh and Vali Bennett, respectively, for being accommodating and understanding of a writer's creative needs. Thank you for never making me choose between doing what's best for me as a writer and what's best for me as a person who needs a paycheque for general life things like food.

To my grandmother, Evelyn, thank you for your assistance throughout my schooling and for your faith in my talent.

Finally, I would like to thank my mother: my number one fan, my very first reader. Thank you for your unwavering support of my ambition, for never wanting me to be anything other than what I am. Thank you for demanding excellence from me and for doing everything you could to help turn my passion into an actuality, from getting me a rhyming dictionary when I wrote songs and poems in junior high to telling me about creative writing classes and workshops to take in undergrad. I am forever grateful.

ZALIKA REID-BENTA is a Toronto-based writer whose work has appeared on CBC Books, in *TOK: Writing the New Toronto*, and in *Apogee Journal*. In 2011, George Elliott Clarke recommended her as a "Writer to Watch." She received a Master of Fine Arts in fiction from Columbia University in 2014 and is an alumna of the 2017 Banff Centre Writing Studio. She is currently working on a young-adult fantasy novel, drawing inspiration from Jamaican folklore and Akan spirituality.

Bringing a book from manuscript to what you are reading is a team effort.

Dialogue Books would like to thank everyone at Little, Brown who helped to publish *Frying Plantain* in the UK.

Editorial
Sharmaine Lovegrove
Sophia Schoepfer
Thalia Proctor
Amy Baxter

Contracts
Anniina Vuori

Sales
Caitriona Row
Ben Goddard
Rachael Hum
Hannah Methuen
Andrew Cattanach

Design
Nick Evans
Jo Taylor
Helen Bergh

Production
Narges Nojoumi

Publicity
Millie Seaward

Marketing
Emily Moran
Hillary Tisman
Hermione Ireland